Praise for *The Scarlet Circus*

"For this whimsical collection, World Fantasy Award winner Yolen (*The Midnight Circus*) brings together 11 fantastical shorts centered on romantic love. Yolen's trademark fairy tale styling is on display throughout, with vivid, pithy prose animating each quirky flight of fancy. In her author's note, she complains that dictionary definitions of romance are all too 'human-centric.' Indeed, these tales feature romance between all manner of magical creatures: a fey man falls for a ghost in the comic 'Dusty Loves,' though she's more interested in haunting the boy she left behind; a sailor witnesses the love between a family of merpeople in the sweet 'The Sea Man'; a princess meets a man who may or may not be a unicorn in standout 'The Unicorn Hunt'; and an enslaved man finds romance with a djinn in the dated 'Memoirs of a Bottle Djinn,' the weakest piece. Many stories riff on the familiar: 'The Sword and the Stone' offers a fresh take on King Arthur, while 'Peter in Wonderland' imagines an adult Alice falling down the rabbit hole again."
—*Publishers Weekly*

"*The Scarlet Circus* is a magical collection of love stories, where love is often an act of courage and intelligence. Jane Yolen has a true storyteller's voice—a voice that makes the writing disappear so that only the stories remain."
—Anne Bishop, *New York Times* bestselling author of the Black Jewels series

"All these years, and Jane Yolen still reduces me to helpless, gibbering admiration. I'll read anything with her name on it, even if it's just a damn grocery list!"
—Peter S. Beagle, author of *In Calabria*

"Jane Yolen spins captivating tales of whimsy, romance, brave knights, dragons, and twist endings. It was like reading the Grimm's fairy tales as a kid—it has that same timeless feel. I was immersed in every story."
—Heather Wallwork, author of *Entwined*

"Jane Yolen is not only one of the best writers I know of, she's also *consistently* excellent. A Grand Master, old-school style!"
—Mercedes Lackey, author of the Valdemar series

"*The Scarlet Circus* is a magnificent and beautiful anthology from a master storyteller! Jane Yolen's stories and poems reach directly into your heart and fill you with the loveliest kind of magic. I absolutely adored it!"
—Sarah Beth Durst, award-winning author of The Queens of Renthia series

"*The Scarlet Circus* is a charming bouquet of love stories from a heady array of fantastical viewpoints. Here be magic, and romance."
—Susan Palwick, author of *All Worlds Are Real*

5/5 stars. "This isn't your typical romance novel though.

That romance has a broad definition and doesn't always have a happy ending. In fact, some of the stories are quite dark. I really like it when Jane Yolen takes a story you think you know and turns it on its head."
—*The Neverending TBR List*

Praise for Jane Yolen

"The Hans Christian Andersen of America."
—*Newsweek*

"The Aesop of the twentieth century."
—*The New York Times*

"Jane Yolen is a gem in the diadem of science fiction and fantasy."
—*Analog*

"One of the treasures of the science fiction community."
—Brandon Sanderson, author of the Mistborn series

"Jane Yolen facets her glittering stories with the craft of a master jeweler."
—Elizabeth Wein, author of *Code Name Verity*

"There is simply no better storyteller working in the fantasy field today. She's a national treasure."
—Terri Windling, author of *The Wood Wife* and *The Essential Bordertown*

"These Tachyon volumes are an invaluable reminder of Yolen's central role in contemporary fantasy, and perhaps an equally invaluable starting point for readers."
—*Locus* on *The Emerald Circus* and *How to Fracture a Fairy Tale*

Also by Jane Yolen

Novels

The Wizard of Washington Square (1969)
Hobo Toad and the Motorcycle Gang (1970)
The Bird of Time (1971)
The Magic Three of Solatia (1974)
The Transfigured Hart (1975)
The Mermaid's Three Wisdoms (1978)
The Acorn Quest (1981)
The Stone Silenus (1984)
Cards of Grief (1985)
The Devil's Arithmetic (1988)
The Dragon's Boy (1990)
Wizard's Hall (1991)
Briar Rose (1992)
Good Griselle (1994)
The Wild Hunt (1995)
The Sea Man (1997)
Here There Be Ghosts (1998)
Sword of the Rightful King (2003)
The Young Merlin Trilogy: Passager, Hobby, and Merlin (2004)
Except the Queen (with Midori Snyder, 2010)
Snow in Summer (2011)
Curse of the Thirteenth Fey (2012)
B. U. G. (Big Ugly Guy) (with Adam Stemple, 2013)
Centaur Rising (2014)
A Plague of Unicorns (2014)
Trash Mountain (2015)
The Last Tsar's Dragons (with Adam Stemple, 2019)
Arch of Bone (2021)

Collections

The Girl Who Cried Flowers and Other Tales (1974)
The Moon Ribbon (1976)
The Hundredth Dove and Other Tales (1977)
Dream Weaver (1979)
Neptune Rising: Songs and Tales of the Undersea People (1982)
Tales of Wonder (1983)
The Whitethorn Wood and Other Magicks (1984)
Dragonfield and Other Stories (1985)
Favorite Folktales from Around the World (1986)
Merlin's Booke (1986)
The Faery Flag (1989)
Storyteller (1992)
Here There Be Dragons (1993)
Here There Be Unicorns (1994)
Among Angels (with Nancy Willard, 1995)
Here There Be Witches (1995)
Here There Be Angels (1996)
Twelve Impossible Things Before Breakfast (1997)
Here There Be Ghosts (1998)
Not One Damsel in Distress (2000)
Sister Emily's Lightship and Other Stories (2000)
Mightier Than the Sword (2003)
Once Upon A Time (She Said) (2005)
The Last Selchie Child (2012)

Grumbles from the Forest: Fairy-Tales Voices with a Twist (with Rebecca Kai Dotlich, 2013)
The Emerald Circus (2017)
How to Fracture a Fairy Tale (2018)
The Midnight Circus (2020)

Graphic Novels
Foiled (2010)
The Last Dragon (2011)
Curses! Foiled Again (2013)

Young Heroes series (with Robert J. Harris)
Odysseus in the Serpent Maze (2001)
Hippolyta and the Curse of the Amazons (2002)
Atalanta and the Arcadian Beast (2003)
Jason and the Gorgon's Blood (2004)

A Rock 'n' Roll Fairy Tale Series
Pay the Piper (with Adam Stemple, 2005)
The Troll Bridge (with Adam Stemple, 2006)
Boots and the Seven Leaguers (2000)

The Seelie Wars Series (with Adam Stemple)
The Hostage Prince (2013)
The Last Changeling (2014)
The Seelie King's War (2016)

Stone Man Mysteries (with Adam Stemple):
Stone Cold (2016)
Sanctuary (2018)
Breaking Out the Devil (2019)

Pit Dragon Chronicles Series
Dragon's Blood (1982)
Heart's Blood (1984)
A Sending of Dragons (1988)
Dragon's Heart (2009)

Tartan Magic
The Pictish Child (1999)
The Wizard's Map (1999)
The Bagpiper's Ghost (2002)

Books of the Great Alta
Sister Light, Sister Dark (1988)
White Jenna (1989)
The One-Armed Queen (1998)

THE SCARLET CIRCUS

JANE YOLEN

THE SCARLET CIRCUS
NEBULA AWARD-WINNING AUTHOR
JANE YOLEN
INTRODUCTION BY BRANDON SANDERSON
TACHYON
SAN FRANCISCO

The Scarlet Circus

Interior and cover design by Elizabeth Story

Tachyon Publications LLC
1459 18th Street #139
San Francisco, CA 94107
415.285.5615
www.tachyonpublications.com
tachyon@tachyonpublications.com

Series Editor: Jacob Weisman
Project Editor: Jaymee Goh

Print ISBN: 978-1-61696-386-6
Digital ISBN: 978-1-61696-387-3

Printed in the United States by Versa Press, Inc.

First Edition: 2023
9 8 7 6 5 4 3 2 1

CONTENTS

Story Notes and Poems

INTRODUCTION

Brandon Sanderson

Today, I address two audiences.

Some of you know what you're in for by picking up this book. You are a fan of Jane's work already, and may have been waiting for this collection.

In that case, I can tell you, this book is exactly what you want. Eclectic, powerful, beautiful, and passionate. It is themed toward romance, yes, but I have yet to read a Jane Yolen story without a hint of romance—some by the classical definition taught in English classes, others by the newer one that involves more kissing. In truth, this is another wildly eclectic collection of stories, tied together by Jane's own brand of genius as much as it is by any theme.

If you're already a fan, though, why are you reading my words? Skip this introduction. Her words are waiting for you. You're in for a treat.

But there's another audience here. Someone picking

up this book while browsing. Maybe you know some of Jane's other work, and are curious. Maybe you just happened across this volume by chance. I want to speak to that reader in particular. Because you . . . you're in for the *real* treat.

You get to dive in unaware.

I had this experience as a youth. Unlike a lot of writers, I wasn't much of a reader when I was a kid. I discovered fantasy as a genre when I was fourteen, got sucked in, and turned into the person I am. Usually, that's all I say about the story—but it has an addendum. Because while I didn't discover fantasy as a genre until I was fourteen, there was one special book I discovered far earlier than that. It was a Jane Yolen novel.

The first book in my entire life I can ever remember loving—truly loving—was Jane's masterpiece *Dragon's Blood*. I was in grade school, maybe ten years old, when I found that book. I wouldn't call it a middle-grade novel. Indeed, I'd say that *Dragon's Blood*—like much of Jane's work—transcends age categories and genre.

In this book I found something special that spoke to me, but I didn't consider myself to be a "reader." And so, I moved on. But years later, when I finally discovered there was an entire genre of similar stories, it was the echoes of Jane's work that convinced me to join the fantasy fold. In so doing, her work changed—in the most literal sense—my entire life. Some of you reading this might be familiar with my work. I say that in a very real way, without Jane Yolen, I very well might never have become a writer.

(To that end, one of the prized possessions of my collection is a signed copy of *Dragon's Blood*, in which Jane wrote "For Brandon, the book that did him in.")

But what was it that I loved about that book, and what I continue to love about Jane's work? What is it you're going to find in this volume to love as well? Well, art is famously difficult to define in simple terms. The colors just tend to bleed out over our words and make a sloppy mess of it all. I'll try anyway.

I think the most enduring and appealing aspect of Jane's work is her ability to mash together whimsy and poignancy. Most of us come to works of the fantastic with a built-in desire for whimsy—for worldbuilding, enchantment, the chance to go someplace new and exciting. Yet, whimsy is a fleeting emotion. The will-o'-the-wisp of human experience. Often it peeks in to distract, then leaves just as quickly.

Great fantasy fiction frequently takes that initial hook of interest, then uses it to say something. Not in a "billboard in your face" way—rather in a "Huh. I need to think about that" way. I don't think I've ever walked away from one of Jane's stories without wanting to talk to someone about it.

Beyond that, there's her breadth. In vocal musical performance, we'll often talk about a singer's range. The number of octaves they can hit, the versatility of their voice. I find this something we under-appreciate in the fiction world. And if you want to talk about proof of a writer's range . . . well, you're holding one.

I don't know of another author who can so fluidly

move from bestselling picture books about tired dinosaurs, to powerful stories targeted at teens, to stylistically and thematically challenging stories that command adult science fiction and fantasy's top honors. Jane has an entire closet full of hats she wears, and this collection managed to surprise even me—a longtime fan—with her versatility as a storyteller.

That's the true fun of a collection like this. You don't know what's coming next, only that it's going to be some different shade of brilliant from the story before it. And so, for those who have picked up this volume on a lark, let me say that I envy you for the ride you're going to get to take. I wish I could discover her stories for the first time again myself. Turn the page, and be delighted.

But fair warning, you might want to pick up two copies. Because once you're done reading, you're going to want to talk to someone else about what you've been reading.

A LITTLE BIT OF LOVING

Jane Yolen

When asked what I write by researchers, interviewers, school children, adult audiences, and people I meet at conferences, I normally answer, "Everything!" But then I hesitate charmingly and add, "Except sport stories, cowboy stories, and romance novels."

But I am lying. (Definition of an author/storyteller = liar. It runs in the family.)

You see, I have published well over 400 books, plus thousands of poems and a huge basket load of stories. So when I really want to parse that answer, I need to think about my output. And then I remember that way back in the '60s/'70s/'80s, I published two children's picture books about baseball. So, yeah, I have written sport stories.

Even earlier, I wrote a children's picture book about the wild(ish) west. It had tumbleweeds and all.

But no romance novels. When asked about that, I reply: "I am in my mid-eighties. The research alone would likely kill me."

However, I have a brand-new husband after fifteen years of widowhood . . . who knew!!! And there is a lot of "interesting" research on love and love affairs available, and I have spent years on other research projects (including three Holocaust novels), none of which have killed me.

But that begs another question: I am also forgetting the many short stories and poems in the SF/fantasy genre that I have published over the years in magazines, collections, and anthologies, many of which have a romantic tinge or a full-out romantic assault as the through-line. Yeah—not romance novels, but a lot of romance all the same. Many of those stories (my favorites) you will find in this book.

And I have also written songs of love as well, a number of which have been performed by bands.

The difference is that these stories are either science fictional or fairy tale-ish or fantastical. Humans fall in love with mermaids or mermen, or selchies or fairies or half-breed redcaps, or magical birds or magicians or . . . hard to rule anything out when you write genre.

And, come to think of it, some of my SF and fantasy novels include long and involved romantic storylines, like *Briar Rose* which is based on the fairy tale but set in the Holocaust, or like the Great Alta Saga that has magic and a prince, or like *The Curse of the Thirteenth Fey*, which is full of fairies (not the little people with wings kind though), or like *Except the Queen*, co-written with Midori Snyder, and that book includes a romance between a couple of middle-aged fairies and humans.

OMG—I HAVE written romance novels. Turns out I am a complete romantic! Who knew!

However, please note: there's a difference between "romantic novels" and capital-R Romance Novel. The former has a measure of love story woven into its arc (think of *War and Peace*) but it is not just about the love story . . . or the lovers that you thought it was going to be about. But a Romance novel is driven entirely by the love story, even though there may be a decoration of history draped over its shoulders. The Romance Writers Association's definition of the genre, which is capital-R Romance, is quite specific: "a central love story and an emotionally satisfying and optimistic ending." As you can see, they are quite rigid in the happily-ever-after aspect expected in each novel, whereas the stories in this book may have sad endings, compromised endings, or joyous ones. In other words, real life. Except also magical and fantastical and science fictional . . . of course.

So, I guess I have to redirect those questions from researchers, interviewers, et al to say that I have written fantastical stories and books that include Romance as well as True Love, with a bit of snogging and touching and kissing and other stuff. And if this makes me a writer of Romance Books, then perhaps we need to redefine the concept, not redefine me.

So—here's a challenge: using a few common definitions of love and romance culled from the internet, how do they wrap their loving arms around the stories in this book?

Here is Google's definition: "A feeling of excitement and mystery associated with love." What about how I love my Prius? My dog? Or my grandkids? My country? No romance here but still love.

This is Wikipedia's basic definition: "Romance or romantic love is a feeling of love for, or a strong attraction towards another person, and the courtship behaviors undertaken by an individual to express those overall feelings." The term "person" is so human-centric. What about those selchies and mermaids and . . . ?

The Wikipedia entry also includes this definition from the *Wiley Blackwell Encyclopedia of Family Studies*: "Romantic love, based on the model of mutual attraction and on a connection between two people that bonds them as a couple, creates the conditions for overturning the model of family and marriage that it engenders." Why just people? Why just two? And again, we have a human-centric idea (and ideal) of a love relationship. Building a family when one of the partners is a selchie or a mermaid or a redcap means having to redefine—through story—the definition of love (and also the definition of "people"? Lots of science fiction romances count the nonhuman as "people"). Of family. Of sex or contentment or passion. Or release.

However, I am a storyteller, not a sex counselor. I am not writing these stories to help anyone, or to lecture on how to create a permanent relationship with a ghoul, or have an extramarital affair with a ghost. I am simply telling a story. If along the way it entertains, amuses, even arouses, or touches the reader deeply, then my work is well done.

If the story teaches you how to make love, have sex, or find a magical partner—well, that's additional and not intended. These stories are entertainment, not textbook. And yes, I do know that stories can be great teachers. But it is a byproduct, not the reason for their existence.

I am often asked to name my favorite stories in a collection of mine, as if my favorites have anything to do with my readers' favorites. My choices are often a combination of how hard or easily the piece slipped through my fingers onto the keys or how the story speaks about a particular moment in my life.

In the case of the stories here in *Scarlet Circus*, what resonates most with me right now are two stories that speak to two different kinds of love: one familial, centered in a long marriage to my late husband, and the other to my second marriage after a fifteen-year-long widowship.

"The Sea Man" was based on a bit from a log by a seventeenth century Dutch Captain who wrote that the crew had captured a merman or zee man and who was eventually rescued by his wife and family's appearance. I suspect there had been much drinking before the log was written. The story was written when my first husband David was alive and well, and it celebrates the closeness of family and how we are all important within that group.

The other story, "A Ghost of an Affair," reflects my solid and wonderful second marriage. For the story is about finding a lost lover from the past. The story was written way before we re-met, but my new husband and I dated for two months in college and spent those two months talking about poetry, especially Emily Dickinson. A very non-romantic romance. But we have re-met, both of us widowed, and fallen deeply in love which means we need to revisit both past and present in order to make a good future.

So there you have it . . . almost.

Along the way to writing this introduction, a poem fell out of my fingers. Yes, this often happens. It is a gift, not a curse. But it explains all of the above in a different way.

However, if you are wired to using poetry as an introduction, I offer it here. But I do so with the knowledge that poetry is a foreign language to some, an old friend and comfort to others, and can be a revelation to the chosen few.

"Falling in Love with the Other"

For some the other
is the opposite sex,
the binary or the nonbinary,
the several or the one.
It can be the person in the mirror,
whose smile is on the wrong side,
a dog, cat, hawk, guinea pig.
It can be the unbelievable—

a merman, tailed and taut,
Merlin in the tree's embrace,
a dark angel with wings enfolding,
or an old man who speaks poems
into your ready ear.
You are chooser and chosen.
It can be for an hour,
or a year,
or whatever forever
is in your contract,
signed, spoken, unspoken,
clear, unclear.
Or imprinted on the heart.

SANS SOLEIL

There once was a prince called Sans Soleil, which is to say, Sunless. It had been prophesied at his birth that he would grow so handsome, his beauty would outshine the sun. That he might not be killed by the jealous star, he had to be kept in the dark, for it was said that he would die if ever a shaft of sunlight fell upon his brow.

So the very night he was born, his father, the king, had him carried away to a castle that was carved out of rock. And in that candlelit cave-castle, the young prince grew and flourished without ever seeing the sun.

Now, by the time Sans Soleil was twenty years old, the story of his strange beauty and of the evil prediction had been told at every hearth and hall in the kingdom. And every maiden of marrying age had heard his tragic tale.

But one in particular, Viga, the daughter of a duke, did not believe what she heard.

"Surely," she said, tossing her raven-black hair from her face, "surely the king has hidden his son from the light because he is too monstrous to behold."

Her father shook his head. "Nay," he replied. "I have been to this cave-castle and have seen this prince. He is handsomer than the sun."

But still Viga did not believe what her father told her. "The sun cannot harm anyone," she said. "There is no sense in what you say." And she took herself to the king dressed in her finest gown of silver and gold.

"Sire," she said, "at court you have been taken in by lies. The sun is not harmful. It nourishes. It causes all things to grow. It will not kill the prince."

The king was touched by the girl's sincerity. He was moved by her beauty. He was awed by her strength of purpose, for it is no little thing to contradict a king. Still, he shook his head and said, "It was prophesied at his birth that he would die if ever a shaft of sunlight struck his brow."

"Old wives and young babes believe such tales. They should not frighten you, sire. They do not frighten me," Viga replied.

"They do not frighten you because you are not the one who would die," said the king, and at these words all the courtiers smiled and nodded their heads and murmured to one another. "Still, I will give the matter more thought."

Viga gave a low curtsy. And as she rose, she said quietly, so that only the king could hear it, "It does seem strange that sun and son do sound the same." Then she smiled brightly and departed.

The king was true to his word and gave the matter more thought. And what he concluded was this: that his son and Viga should be wed. For he liked her courage and admired her beauty, and thought she would make his son a most suitable wife. So the king and the duke set the wedding date for a week from the following night.

When the night was deep and no spot of sun still lit the kingdom, a carriage with drawn curtains arrived at Viga's door. Out stepped the handsomest man she had ever seen. He was dressed all in red and gold, like the sun.

They were wed by candlelight, and their golden rings were carved with images of the sun. There was feasting and dancing till three. Then the two talked and kissed far into the night, as befits a couple who are but newly wed.

But at the crowing of the village cocks announcing that the sun would soon rise, Sans Soleil stood up. "I must go. I cannot allow the sun to shine upon me."

"Do not leave me," Viga said. "Now that we are wed. I cannot bear to have you away from my sight. Do not be afraid of the sun. It will not harm you. Stay here with me."

"No, I am safe only in my cave. You are my wife; come and live in my cave-castle with me."

"Live in a cave?" said Viga. "Never."

So the prince tore himself from her grasp and ran out into the waiting golden carriage. With a crack of the whip, the horses were away before the sun could gain the sky.

However, Viga was a woman of strong will. So determined was she to prove to Sans Soleil that she was right and he would not be killed by the sun, she devised a plan. That very day she sent her maidservants to buy up all the cockerels in the kingdom. Then she had her footmen bind the birds and throw them down into the duke's deepest dungeons, where it would always be dark as night.

But there was one rooster the servants could not buy, the pet of the potter's boy. The child cried so much at the thought of losing his bird, his father would not part with it.

"What is one cockerel out of so many?" the servants asked themselves. And so they neglected to tell their mistress of the last bird.

That evening again Sans Soleil's carriage came to Viga's door. As before, the prince was dressed all in red and gold like the sun, and the feathers on his cap stood out like golden ray. In his hand he carried a sunburst, a ruby brooch with beams like a star.

"This is my only sun," he said to Viga. "Now it is yours."

And they forgave one another for the harsh words of the morn. They touched and kissed as married couples do, far into the night.

At the coming of the dawn, far off in the village, the cockerel belonging to the potter's child began to crow.

"Is that a cockerel I hear?" asked Sans Soleil, sitting up.

"There is no cockerel," replied Viga sleepily, for she thought indeed there was none.

But again the rooster crowed out, and, hearing no answering call from his brothers, he sang out louder than before.

"I am sure I hear the warning of the sun's approach," said Soleil.

"It is nothing but a servant's snore," Viga replied. "Stay quiet. Stay asleep. Stay with me."

But on the third crow, Sans Soleil leaped up. "I must go," he said. "I cannot allow the sun to shine upon me."

"Do not put your faith in such old wives' tales," cried Viga. "The sun cannot hurt you. Put your faith in me."

But it was too late. The prince was gone, running down into his golden carriage and away to his cave-castle before the sun could start up in the sky.

However, Viga was a woman of strong will and passion. She was determined not to lose her lover for a single day because of such a foolish tale. She was convinced that if the prince but forgot the sun, he would learn that it could do him no harm. So she decided to have the last rooster put in her father's dungeon.

But she did not trust her servants anymore. With her cloak wrapped about her and covering her face with a sleeve, Viga slipped out into the streets. By the potter's hut she saw the bird strutting and preening its feathers in the sun.

Quickly, she looked around, but there was no one in sight. She reached down, snatched up the cockerel, and hid it under her cloak. In the night of her garment the bird made no sound.

She was back in her own home before the potter's child could set up his wail. The cockerel she put with its brothers in the dark. Then she waited impatiently for the sun to set that she might see her lover again.

That evening, so great was his haste, Sans Soleil himself drove the golden carriage to the door. He leaped to the ground and in a graceful bound ran to the waiting girl.

They ate and touched and sang and danced and talked until the night was through. But there were no cockerels to crow and warn them of the dawn.

Suddenly the prince glanced out of the window. "It is becoming light," he cried. "I must leave. You know that I cannot allow the sun to shine on me."

"Love me. Trust me. Stay with me," said Viga, smoothing his hair with her strong hands.

But Sans Soleil glanced out of the window again. "Is that the sun? Tell me, for I have never seen it shine."

Viga smoothed his neck with her fingers. "Forget your foolish fears. The sun nourishes. It does not kill. Stay with me here and greet the dawn."

The prince was moved by her plea and by his love for her. But just as he was about to stay, fear, like an old habit, conquered him. He jumped up and blinked at the light. "I must go to my cave. Only there will I be safe," he cried. And before she could stop him, he tore from her grasp and sped out into the dawn.

Viga ran after him. "Do not be afraid," she called. Her long black hair streamed out behind her like the rays of a black star. "It is but a tale. A tale for children. *You* are the sun."

But the prince did not hear her. As he ran out into the courtyard, the sun rose in full brilliance over the wall. Sans Soleil had never seen anything so glorious before. He stood and stared at the burning star. The sunlight struck him full in the face. And with a single cry of pain or anger or regret, he fell down dead.

Viga saw him fall. She cried out, "Oh, Sans Soleil, it was true. Who would have believed it? Now it is I who am sunless, for you were my sun."

She threw herself upon his still form, her breast against his, her cool white brow on the ashes of his, and wept.

The next year, in the courtyard where Sans Soleil had fallen, a single sunflower grew. But unlike others of its kind, it bloomed all year round and always turned its face away from the sun.

Viga had a belvedere built around it. There she spent her days, tending the flower, watering it, and turning its soil.

When visitors arrived at her father's house, she would tell them the story of her love for Sans Soleil. And the story always ended with this caution: "Sometimes," Viga would say, "what we believe is stronger than what is true."

DUSTY LOVES

There is an ash tree in the middle of our forest on which my brother Dusty has carved the runes of his loves. Like the rings of its heartwood, the tree's age can be told by the number of carvings on its bark. *Dusty loves . . .* begins the legend high up under the first branches. Then the litany runs like an old tale down to the tops of the roots. Dusty has had many, many loves, for he is the romantic sort. It is only in taste that he is wanting.

If he had stuck to the fey, his own kind, at least part of the time, Mother and Father would not have been so upset. But he had a passion for princesses and milkmaids, that sort of thing. The worst, though, was the time he fell in love with the ghost of a suicide at Miller's Cross. *That* is a story indeed.

It began quite innocently, of course. All of Dusty's affairs do. He was piping in the woods at dawn, practicing his solo for the Solstice. Mother and Father prefer that he does his scales and runs as far from our pavilion as possible, for his notes excite the local wood doves, and the place is stained quite enough as it *is*. Ever dutiful, Dusty packed his pipes and a cress sandwich and made for a Lonely Place. Our forest has many such: dells silvered with dew, winding streams bedecked with morning mist, paths twisting between blood-red trilliums—all the accoutrements of Faerie. And when they are not cluttered with bad poets, they are really quite nice. But Dusty preferred human highways and byways, saying that such busy places were, somehow, the loneliest places of all. Dusty always had a touch of the poet himself, though his rhymes were, at best, slant.

He had just reached Miller's Cross and perched himself atop a standing stone, one leg dangling across the Anglo-Saxon inscription, when he heard the sound of human sobbing. There was no mistaking it. Though we fey are marvelous at banshee wails and the low-throbbing threnodies of ghosts, we have not the ability to give forth that half gulp, half cry that is so peculiar to humankind, along with the heaving bosom and the wetted cheek.

Straining to see through the early-morning fog, Dusty could just make out an informal procession heading down the road toward him. So he held his breath—which, of course, made him invisible, though it never works for long—and leaned forward to get a better view.

There were ten men and women in the group, six of them carrying a coffin. In front of the coffin was a priest in his somber robes, an iron cross dangling from a chain. The iron made Dusty sneeze, for he is allergic and he became visible for a moment until he could catch his breath again. But such was the weeping and carryings-on below him, no one even noticed.

The procession stopped just beneath his perch, and Dusty gathered up his strength and leaped down, landing to the rear of the group. At the moment his feet touched the ground, the priest had—fortuitously—intoned, "Dig!" The men had set the coffin on the ground and begun. They were fast diggers, and the ground around the stone was soft from spring rains. Six men and six spades make even a deep grave easy work, though it was hardly a pretty sight, and far from the proper angles. And all the while they were digging, a plump lady in gray worsted, who looked upholstered rather than dressed, kept trying to fling herself into the hole. Only the brawny arms of her daughters on either side and the rather rigid stays of her undergarments kept her from accomplishing her gruesome task.

At last the grave was finished, and the six men lowered the coffin in while the priest sprinkled a few unkind words over the box, words that fell on the ears with the same thudding foreboding as the clods of earth upon the box. Then they closed the grave and dragged the weeping women down the road toward the town.

Now Dusty, being the curious sort, decided to stay. He let out his breath once the mourners had turned their backs on him, and leaped up onto his perch again. Then he began to practice his scales with renewed vigor, and had even gotten a good hold on the second portion of "Puck's Sarabande" when the moon rose. Of course, the laws of the incorporeal world being what they are, the ghost of the suicide rose, too. And that was when Dusty fell in love.

She was unlike her sisters, being petite and dark where they had been large and fair. She had two dimples, one that could be seen when she frowned and one when she smiled. Her hair was plaited with white velvet ribands and tied off with white baby's breath, which, if she had not been dead and a ghost, would have certainly been wilted by then. There was a fringe of dark hair almost obscuring the delicate arch of her eyebrows. Her winding sheet became her.

Dusty jumped down and bowed low. She was so new at being a ghost, she was startled by him. Though he is tall for an elf, he is small compared to most humans and rarely startles anyone. It is the ears, of course, that give him away. That, and the fact that, like most male feys, he is rather well endowed. The fig leaf was invented for human vanity. The solitary broad-leafed gingko was made for the fey. She covered her eyes with her hands, which, of course, did not help, since she could see right through her palms, bones and all.

"What are you?" she whispered. And then she added plaintively, "What am I?"

"You are dead," Dusty said. "And I am in love." (Foreplay being a word found only in human dictionaries.)

But the ghost turned from him and began to weep. "Alas," she cried, "then it was all for naught, for where is my sweet Roman?"

Dusty tried again: "I will play Roman for you. Or even Greek." He will promise anything when he is in the early throes of love.

But the ghost only wept the dry tears of the dead, crying, "Roman is the name of the man I love. Where is he?"

"Obviously alive and well and pursuing other maidens," said Dusty, his forthright nature getting in the way of his wooing. "For if he were dead, he would be here with you. But *I* am here."

He tried to enfold her in his arms, but she slipped away as easily as mist.

"Are you, then, dead?" she asked.

"I am of the fey," he said.

But if she listened, it was not apparent, for she continued as if answers were not a part of conversation. "He must be dead. I saw him die. It is why *I* died. To be with him."

That, of course, decided Dusty. He was always a fool for lost causes. And I must say, from my readings of history, that I knew we would all have to watch him carefully in the 1780s, the 1860s, and the 1930s, 1950s, 1970s, and 1990s.

"Tell me, gracious lady," he said, careful to speak the elfin equivalent of the Shouting Voice, which is to say, well-modulated. At that level the voice could bring milk from a maiden's breast, cause graybeards to dance, and stir love in even the coldest heart.

But the suicide's ghost seemed immune. She wrung her hands into vapor, but did not step an inch closer to Dusty's outstretched arms. Sometimes the voice works, and sometimes it does not.

So, shrugging away his disappointment, Dusty tried again, this time in a more natural tone. "Start from the beginning. I may have missed something important, coming in the middle like this."

The ghost settled herself daintily some three feet above the ground, crossed her ankles prettily, and offered him her smiling dimple, "My name is . . . or was . . . oh, how *do* these things work in the afterlife?"

"Do not worry about niceties," Dusty said, patting her hand and the air beneath it at the same time. "Just begin already." (I do believe it was this moment he began falling out of love. But he will never admit to that.)

She sniffled angelically and pouted, showing him the other dimple. "My name is Julie. And I was in love . . . am in love . . . oh, dear!" She began to cry anew.

Dusty offered a webkerchief to her. She reached for it, and it fell between them, for, of course, she could no more touch it then Dusty could touch her. She wiped her nose, instead, on the winding sheet.

"Go on," Dusty said, blushing when she looked at him with gratitude. He often mistook such human emotions as gratitude, sympathy, and curiosity for love.

"My own true love is Roman. It is a family name, but I like it."

"A fine name," Dusty agreed hastily, having bitten back the response that children should be named after natural things like sunshine, dust, and rainbows, not inanimates like cities, countries, and empires.

Warming to her tale, Julie, the ghost, began to catalog her own true love's charms, an adolescent litany of cheeks, hair, muscles, and thews that anyone but another adolescent would have found unbearable. As it was, Dusty was as busy listing Julie's charms. They were certainly a pair.

The families, it seems, were feuding. Something about a pig and a poke. Dusty never did get it straight. But the upshot was that Roman's parents would not let him marry Julie, and Julie's parents would not let her marry Roman. Such are the judicious settlements of humankind.

So the two, instead of finding a sensible solution—like moving to Verona, changing their names, or buying both sets of parents new pigs and new pokes—decided on suicide as the answer. Answer! They had not even discovered the right question.

But of course, Dusty agreed with her. Even the fey have hormonal imbalances, which is all that measures the difference between adolescent and adult.

"What you need now," Dusty said in his sensible voice, "is to reunite with your own true love."

Julie began another cascade of tears. "But that is impossible. He is alive. And I am . . . I am . . ."

"Not alive," Dusty said, being as tactful as could be under the circumstances.

"Dead!" Julie finished unhappily, the cascade having become a torrent.

"But you thought he was dead," Dusty said.

"I found him lying in a pool of blood," she answered. "There was blood on his hands and on his face and on his coat and on his . . ." She blushed prettily and hid her face with her hands again.

Dusty admired her shy smile through the transparent bones.

"Everywhere!" she finished.

"Did you look for a wound?" Dusty asked.

"Blood makes me urpy," she admitted.

"'Urpy'?" If her giddiness had not already begun to change his mind, her vocabulary certainly would. *"Urpy?"*

"You know—throw-uppins."

He nodded, looking a bit throw-uppins himself. "So you did not look."

"No. I ran to my nurse and told her I had a headache. A very bad headache. And borrowed a powder. A very strong powder. And . . ."

"And lay down by Roman's side, having drunk the powder in a tisane. Folding your hands over your pretty bosom and spreading your skirts about you like a scallop shell."

She made a moue. "How did you know! Did you see us?"

He sighed. "My sister told me the story. She read it in one of our father's books. His library is vast and has tomes from the from the past and the future as well. Only, I'd better tell you the rest. Roman is not dead."

"Not dead?" She said it with less surprise than before. "How?"

"Who knows? Animal's blood or tomato sauce or spilled wine. Who knows?"

"Roman knows," she said vehemently. Then she stopped. "Why are you laughing?"

How could he explain it to her? Humor is difficult enough between consenting adults. It is impossible interspecies. Dolphins do not trade laughs with wolves, nor do butterflies joke with whales. Puns have a life span half the length of a pratfall. He fell out of love abruptly. But there was still enough attraction left for him to want to help her out.

"You must convince Roman to die," he said. "Only then can he join you."

"How?"

"Haunt him."

Dusty was right, of course. Roman had already begun looking for alternatives. He had a passion for slatterns and sculleries, an interest that had apparently begun long before his dalliance with Julie. She would have been disappointed in him within the course of a normal year—that is, if she had not found him basted like a beef on a platter. Perhaps he had guessed it and had knowingly provoked her into death. If so, Dusty was right about the haunting.

But Julie forgave him, for spirits are so set in their ways. They long for what lingered last. She believed in Roman despite the evidence of her ears and eyes. It led, of course, to a spectacular single-minded haunting.

Poor Roman. He never had a chance. Whenever he was about to place his well-manicured hand upon a maidenly breast, Julie's ghost appeared. She sighed. She swooned. She wailed. She wept. What passion he had, fled. As did the maid to hand.

Dusty enjoyed it all enormously. He coached Julie in every nuance of necromancy: the hollow tones, the fetid breath, the call from beyond the grave. It turned out she had genius for spirit work, a sepulchral flair. Within the week, Roman was on his knees by her grave, begging for release.

Dusty supplied a knife.

Roman ignored it.

Dusty supplied a noose.

Roman ignored it.

Dusty supplied a vial of poison.

Roman joined a monastery, gagged on the plain food, choked on the sweet wine, and longed to talk to his neighbor. He escaped less than a month later over the wall, his habit rucked up around his knees, his sandals in hand.

"Your poor hair," sighed Julie to him as he prostrated himself below the standing stone. The memory of her hand stirred the strand of golden fuzz over his tonsure.

"Give me a month to grow it back, and I will join you, my love," he said, smiling up at her. There was larceny in his smile, though she did not recognize it.

"A month I can wait," she said magnanimously. "Even two. But no more."

Dusty, sitting atop the standing stone, made a face. He might not be able to read a woman's heart, but men were no trouble to him at all.

Within the first month, Roman had converted his inheritance to cash and sailed off with a Portuguese upstart to find a brave new world, leaving Julie far behind. Ghosts, as Roman knew full well, cannot travel over water. Particularly not across a vast sea. But he could not outrun his promise. He died on a foreign shore, a poison dart between his eyes and eaten by cannibals directly after. A windspirit brought us the word. He had died messily, with Julie's name upon his lips. She liked that part.

Julie dictated her story, slightly changed, into the ear of a fine-looking poet some years later. He called her his muse, his dark lady, his spirit guide. That so impressed her, she left off haunting and took up musing with a vengeance.

Dusty went away in disgust and found a compliant milkmaid instead, with soft hands, warm thighs, and a taste for the exotic. But that, of course, is another story and not nearly as interesting or as repeatable.

UNICORN TAPESTRY

Princess Marian was a middle child and middle—she often complained—in everything else. Her older sister, Mildred, was beautiful and about to be married to the emperor, Karlmage. Her younger sister, Margaret, was striking and about to be wed to a neighboring king, Hal. But Marian, middling pretty and middling smart and middling in all her talents, was about to be married to no one. There were simply no eligible royals left in the world.

"Or at least in the world as we know it," said her mother. She was never willing to make a completely definitive statement. She sighed and gazed fondly into Marian's eyes (not blue like Mildred's or green like Margaret's but a sort of middling muddy brown). "They are all either married, engaged, enchanted, or strayed. I am sorry, Em. There's always the convent, you know."

The tears that filled Marian's eyes were the same middling muddy color, until they slid down onto her cheeks, where they became ordinary tears. Marian wiped them away quickly. Princesses are not supposed to cry, at least not where they can be seen. She wasn't sad about the not-marrying part. It had always been her contention that marriage is not necessarily the only thing a princess can do. But she didn't want to be shut away in a convent, not when she didn't have the proper strong beliefs.

Marian left her mother's chamber and trudged slowly down the winding stone stair. She went out a little dark side door, the one that was hidden by a large tapestry. Only Marian and her sisters knew about the door. They had discovered it one day playing catch-as-who-can. The door opened onto a wild part of the vast palace gardens, near an untended lily pool.

Marian was so upset, she picked up a smooth white stone and threw it across the pond. It skipped three times before it sank. "If only stones could grant wishes," she said aloud.

"As-you-will," sang out an undistinguished brown bird on the cherry bough. For such a mud-colored bird, it had quite a lovely voice, clear yet tremulous. "As-you-will." Or at least that is what Marian thought the bird sang.

"What I will," Marian answered back, "is to be kept out of the convent. And I wish that I had something—anything—that distinguishes me. That makes me magical. Or special. Marriage is *not* necessary." She paused. "Though it could be nice."

Then she turned and walked away, feeling a fool for having made a wish upon an ordinary white skipping stone that had sunk with scarcely a ripple, and for having talked back to a totally uninteresting and ordinary bird. *Maybe,* she thought fiercely to herself, *maybe I* do *need to be shut away, and not necessarily in a convent, either.*

She made an angry tour around all the gardens, which took several hours. By then most of her anger had dissipated, so she slipped back past the ivy and through the hidden door.

Once in her own chamber again, Marian did what princesses always do. She worked on her embroidery. It was either that or read a book, and she had read the five leather-bound books she owned almost to shreds. New books would not be ready from the scribes until Fall, and they were sure to be boring treatises on religion or heaven or the duties of royalty. The monkish scribes had no sense of romance. What Marian really would have preferred was to have the minstrel's lays set down on strong parchment that would withstand months of rereading. As a princess, Marian knew she could command no such thing, only as a queen. And it looked as if she would never have that chance.

"Bother," she said, stitching away. This year's production was a unicorn hunt, a picture for each of the twenty dining room chairs. She was on the last one now. The year before it had been a bear hunt; the year before that, a boar.

"A bore indeed," Marian said aloud. Her sisters, being much better seamstresses, got to work on doublets and mantles for their husbands-to-be, or long stomachers for themselves. But Marian, being only middling, muddling gifted, did chairs.

The last piece was a picture of the unicorn in a golden cage, surrounded by blossoming trees, on a millefleur background. She was supposed to follow the cartoons set down by her mother's French designer. But just to make things interesting, she decided to add a tiny bird to one of the trees. "A tiny, undistinguished bird on a cherry bough," she said thoughtfully. Quickly she stitched in its outline.

"As-you-will," sang a cheery voice at her window.

When she looked up, the little brown bird was sitting on the ledge.

"Cheeky!" Marian said to the bird, but she smiled when she said it. Then she looked back to her embroidery. When she put the needle down at last, the bird flew away.

"If I were of a believing nature," she said to herself, "I would think I had *wished* that bird to me." She hesitated for a moment and stared at the patch of embroidered work. The new bit looked less like a bird than a brown lump with a yellow beak. "If I were of a believing nature," she added, "I would be happy living in a convent."

She stood and went down the stairs to dinner, where

she sat, along with her sisters, her little brother (who was heir to the throne), her mother, her father, and fourteen other important folk, on the hunting-of-the-bear chairs. It was, she thought rudely, the best way to view her work.

The next day was one of those horrid days when the rain does not fall but simply fuzzes the air. Everything was as grey as stone and as impenetrable.

All three of the princesses sat in their mother's chamber because it had the best-drawing fire and no ceiling drips. And they talked.

They talked as their needles went in and out, in and out, and Marian talked the most. She thought that if she could only keep talking, she wouldn't feel so put out by the world, with the grey, fuzzy, impenetrable world that offered nothing to her but, possibly, lifetime tenure in a convent.

They spoke of the wars, now some twenty years in the past; they spoke of three local witches who had called up a ghost to confront a murderer at his trial; they spoke of the next-door kingdom's famous giant, who had gout; and they spoke of the coming unicorn hunt. Unicorns, being quite rare, always occasioned a special hunt. Emperor Karlmage and King Hal would both be there. The new embroidered chairs were to celebrate a successful hunt. If Marian was lucky, hunt and embroidery would be finished at the same time. She had one chair to go.

"One!" she chirruped to her sisters.

The queen's minstrel droned over his lute by the window, singing about love. He always sang about love. Or about the death of love, which seemed much the same in his mouth. Marian was thoroughly tired of the subject. She bent her head to her embroidery and saw that the lumpy brown bird had not been improved by the passage of time. She wondered if she should unpick the sorry thing and start again, then decided instead to surround it with a few more blossoms. She was working on the third flower, the color of strawberry cream, when the minstrel's string snapped.

"Bother!" Marian said aloud. The sound had caused her to jump and prick her finger so deeply it bled. The strawberry-cream blossoms got much darker because of it.

Her sisters giggled.

Hastily, the minstrel restrung his lute, but Marian had had enough. "I am going out," she said, popping the hurt finger into her mouth and sucking on it till it stopped hurting.

"It is raining," Margaret pointed out.

Marian removed the finger from her mouth. "It is *always* raining," she said. "Or at least it always rains some, every other day. And I am bored with sewing. And bored with love songs. I am going out."

"To do what?" asked Mildred. "You haven't finished the final chair."

That was the problem. Marian had no plans other than to leave. But she was not about to say so. "That is my secret," she said.

She wrapped herself in a good all-weather cloak and went down into the garden. As she stood by the pool, the rain-soaked air holding her close, something stirred in a nearby tree.

"As-you-will," sang a bird behind her.

She turned and stared at the cherry tree but could not see the bird. It was well hidden behind showy pink blossoms. She was certain the blossoms had not been open the day before. *And* they had been a cream color.

For a moment—only a moment—she considered the chair cover she had just been embroidering, with its blood-spattered flowers, then dismissed the connection. She was, she reminded herself, not of a believing nature. Her memory was just playing tricks.

"As-you-will," the bird sang again.

"Don't you know any other song?" Marian asked peevishly.

As if in answer, the bird trilled a song of such surpassing frills and furbelows that Marian clapped her hands in delight. The bird was *much* better than the queen's minstrel.

"Bravo!" she called to it. And at that the rain began to fall in earnest. Wrapping herself even more tightly in the cloak, Marian ran back to the castle and her mother's warm fire.

All night the rain pattered down and Marian, whose room was the highest in the tower and therefore under the roof, heard every drop. She did not sleep a wink, though her maid snored through till dawn.

As a consequence, Marian finished the final piece of embroidery, squeezed as close to the fire as she dared. It was just as well. The visiting hunters had all arrived in time for last night's dinner, and the informal, raucous meal had lasted well into the hind end of the night.

The queen's minstrel had trotted out all his hunting songs for them, though each song still had much romance and love in it: deer turning into lovely maidens, young women shot by lovers who had mistaken them for swans, and the like. Marian had left midway through a particularly long song, sent away by her mother because she had disgraced them all by yawning, and loudly.

Once in her room, Marian had discovered, much to her chagrin, that she could not sleep. Could not—or would not. It was the same. She decided to substitute embroidery for dreams. She had almost finished the thing, with stem and split stitches and couching, the face of the unicorn set in with the spiral stitch her nanny had taught her and she had never dared use before.

Much to her surprise, her unicorn really looked like a unicorn and not like a sagging deer or a deformed goat. The face, in the spiral stitch, was quite wonderful, with an almost human expression. The horn was outlined with the last of the shimmering silver thread. Only the eyes were not quite right. She couldn't think what color to make them—a deep lapis or lighter azure or perhaps the color of old gold. But when she checked her basket, there was only a muddy-brown thread there and she hated using it. Still, she couldn't very well go into her mother's room or her sisters', looking for thread at this hour.

And when she tucked the last of the brown stitches in, finishing off with a proper knot, she found to her surprise that she liked the brown eyes enormously. In fact she liked the whole thing: the muddy-eyed beast in its golden cage, that gold being repeated in the winking eyes of many of the flowers. She didn't have enough gold left to do a proper halter, so she left the unicorn's neck bare.

Stretching, Marian glanced out of the window. The rains had stopped and it was morning, a weak sun just rising. Everything was shimmering and fresh and green.

She suddenly remembered part of one of the minstrel's songs, something about the lawns of Eden:

Where the original garden thrush
Syllabled all of Paradise
From a hand-painted bush.

That was what the world looked like from her window: clean and new, like the first day of the world. She took a deep breath, and that was when she heard the horn of the master of the hunt. It was a dangerous sound, sharp as a knife, cutting the clean air.

For a moment she glanced down at her embroidery and felt a keen regret for that singular beast with the spiral horn. Then, clutching the piece of cloth, she ran down the stairs. Breakfast would certainly be ready if the men were already out on the hunt.

Breakfast consisted of nightingale eggs boiled in the shell, tiny things that contrasted greatly with the goose eggs similarly cooked. There were fresh forced strawberries and slabs of smoked hams—attesting to the success of the last boar hunt. There were brown breads and white breads and one kind of bread—the cook's specialty, which Marian hated—that was nearly black. She counted three different kinds of cheese, a pot of fresh-churned butter, and preserves that ranged from the bright red of raspberry to the dark plummy color of grape. For those who could not do without it, there was the traditional porridge and, to sweeten it, mashed apples. They never ate so well, even on high feast days, except at the hunt breakfast.

Marian found she was suddenly not hungry. *Perhaps,* she thought, *one needs to sleep and dream in order to feel hunger.* She set the embroidery on the table by her plate. She was all but dozing there when her sisters arrived and noisily sat on either side of her, chattering across her about the day.

Marian listened as if in a dream. They spoke of the handsome mantles their men wore, and of the jangling bells on the horses' harnesses. They commented on the emperor's fine roan stallion and the high color on the cheeks of the master of the hunt.

Suddenly Mildred pounced on the embroidery by Marian's plate. "Em!" she cried. "You've finished."

"Not quite," Margaret said. "The unicorn has no halter. You know it cannot be caught without one. Whatever were you thinking, Em?"

"I ran out of thread and it was late," Marian said, trying not to yawn.

"Let me, then," Mildred said, tucking into her pocket and fishing out a needle and three different shades of gold thread. Then, despite Marian's feeble protests, she chose the fairest of the three and proceeded to stitch in a golden rope about the beast's white neck. The stitches were small and even and, Marian had to reluctantly admit, it was the finest part of the whole piece. Still, there was something she didn't like about it.

"And those eyes!" Margaret said, taking the embroidery out of Mildred's hands. "No self-respecting magic creature has *brown* eyes, Em. Lapis—that's the thing." She dipped into her own pocket and came up with a needle, and thread the color of an early spring sky, as well as a pair of gold scissors. She unpicked the unicorn's brown right eye, quickly sewing in a lovely blue one instead.

"But I *liked* the brown eyes," Marian complained. She tugged the embroidery away from her sister. After breakfast, if she could find a match to the brown, she would try to sew that eye again.

They were still sitting at the table when the master's horn clarioned across a far glade.

"Maybe they have found the unicorn," Mildred said, two spots of color, like old bloodstains, shining on her cheeks.

"Maybe they have killed it!" Margaret added. There was a great deal of excitement in her voice.

Killed. Marian had known all along that the unicorn would be killed, not put in a cage with a yellow ribband around its neck. But somehow, with the piece of embroidery before her, like a cartoon of the actual hunt, the whole thing suddenly seemed horrible. Barbaric. She stared down at the cloth. The unicorn, with its one blue, one brown eye, stared back as if pleading for its life.

"Sister," Marian said, turning to Margaret, "lend me your scissors." She held out her hand and Margaret, without asking why, gave them to her. Quickly, Marian snipped away at the yellow threads, unpicking the gold around the unicorn's neck.

I wish, she thought, but did not say it aloud.

The men came back to the castle in a grim and terrible mood. Three hounds had been maimed and the horses all run to lather. The master of the hunt had taken a fall and his hunting horn, used for years by his father and father's father before him, was smashed beyond repair. The emperor had lost his best bow in a bog.

At the last minute, the unicorn had escaped. Surrounded and at bay, it had unaccountably gotten through the circle of men and horses and dogs and disappeared. The hounds could not find the scent.

"This smells of sorcery," King Hal complained.

"Witchery," added the emperor.

"Magic," said Marian's father, always the agreeable host.

Dinner that night was equally grim. No one noticed the embroidered chairs. Only Marian smiled quietly, looking down at her plate. Only Marian ate a full meal.

Halfway through the serving, there was a commotion in the entryway and suddenly, unannounced, a man entered the hall. He was not handsome, Marian thought, but he was strong limbed, with corded muscles and a beaky nose. His hair looked as if the wind might have had a hand in combing it; his clothes were well traveled and stained.

The emperor looked up from his picked-at dinner. "Malcolm!" he cried. "Cousin! We thought you were dead."

"Or vanished," added King Hal.

They stood and embraced him and brought him to meet their host.

"Have you come to be part of our hunt?" the king asked. "We could use another bow."

"Your hunt is over," Malcolm said. "But mine is just begun." He turned and smiled broadly at Marian and then at the queen. Marian wondered that she had ever thought him not handsome.

The queen nodded back. "I suspect you hunt for a wife, sir. May I commend you to my daughter Marian?"

Marian stood, furious, shaking. *This was too baldly done,* she thought. *Like a piece of meat at the market. The convent might be more to my liking.*

"A lovelier girl you could not find," her father added, which made things worse. Lovelier, indeed, when she was there between Margaret and Mildred! Marian thought to flee, like an animal chased through the woods.

But Malcolm walked to her, blocking her escape. She could not go around him without making a scene. Princesses did not make scenes. One needed to be a queen to do that.

Taking her hand, Malcolm spoke to the room at large. "There will be no marriage if only the king and queen will it," he said. "It is the lady's choice."

He looked directly at her and she noticed, with a start, that his eyes were not the same color. One was muddy brown, the other grey, almost blue. It made him look quite wild, untamed.

Marian thought about the embroidery, about the bird on the ledge, about the blossoms on the cherry bough. She thought about the unpicked golden halter and the lapis eye she'd had no time to change. She thought about the smooth white stone and her wishes.

As she was thinking still, he turned her hand over and kissed her palm. When he looked up, he whispered so that only she could hear him, "As you will, my lady. As you will."

They were married in the late Fall, the trees ablaze with color. In the middle of the ceremony, she thought rather belatedly that belief would serve as well outside the convent walls as in.

She asked for the unicorn chairs as part of her dowry. They are in her castle still.

A GHOST OF AN AFFAIR

1.

Most ghost stories begin or end with a ghost. Not this one. This begins and ends with a love affair. That one of the partners was a ghost has little to do with things, except for a complication or two.

The heart need not be beating to entertain the idea of romance. To think otherwise is to misunderstand the nature of the universe.

To think otherwise is to miscalculate the odds of love.

2.

Andrea Crow did not look at all like her name, being fair-haired and soft-voiced. But she had a scavenger's personality, collecting things with a fierce dedication. As a girl she had collected rocks and stones, denuding her parent's driveway of mica-shining pebbles. As an adolescent she had turned rock collecting into an interest in gemstones. By college she was majoring in geology, minoring in jewelry making. (It was one of those schools so prevalent in the '80s where life experience substituted for any real knowledge. Only a student bent on learning ever learned anything. But perhaps that is true even at Oxford, even at Harvard.)

Andrea's rock-hound passion made her a sucker for young men carrying ropes and pitons, and she learned to scramble up stone faces without thinking of the danger. For a while she even thought she might attempt the Himalayas. But a rock-climbing friend died in an avalanche there, and so she decided going to gem shows was far safer. She was a scavenger, but she wasn't stupid.

The friend who died in the avalanche is not the ghost in this story. That was a dead *girl* friend and Andrea was depressingly straight in her love life.

Andrea graduated from college and began a small jewelry business in Chappaqua with a healthy jump-start from her parents who died suddenly in a car crash going home from her graduation. They left a tidy sum and their house to Andrea who, after a suitable period of mourning, plunged into work, turning the garage into her workroom.

She sold her jewelry at craft fairs and Renaissance faires and to several of the large stores around the country who found her Middle Evils line especially charming.

The silver and gold work was superb, of course. She had been well trained. But it was the boxing of the jewelry—in polished rosewood with gold or silver hinges—as well as the printed legends included with each piece that made her work stand out.

Still, her business remained small until one Christmas Neiman Marcus ordered five thousand adder stone rings in Celtic-scrolled rosewood boxes. The rings, according to legend, "ensured prosperity, repelled evil spirits, and in seventeenth-century Scotland were considered to keep a child free of the whooping cough." She finished that order so far in the black that she only had to go to one Renaissance faire the following summer for business.

Well, to be honest, she would have gone anyway. She needed the rest after the Neiman Marcus push. Besides, she enjoyed the faire. Many of her closest friends were there.

All of her closest friends were there.

All three of them.

3.

Simon Morrison was the son and grandson and great-grandson of Crail fisherfolk. He was born to the sea. But the sea was not to his liking. And as he had six brothers born ahead of him who could handle the fishing lines and nets, he saw no reason to stay in Crail for longer than was necessary.

So on the day of his majority, June 17, 1847, he kissed his mother sweetly and said farewell to his father's back, for he was not so big that his da—a small man with a great hand—might not have whipped him for leaving.

Simon took the northwest road out of Crail and made his way by foot to the ferry that crossed the River Forth and so on into Edinburgh. And there he could have lost himself in the alehouses, as had many a lad before him.

But Simon was not just *any* lad. He was a lad with a passionate dream. And while it was not his father's and grandfather's and great-grandfather's dream of herring by the hundredweight, it was a dream nonetheless.

His dream was to learn to work in silver and gold. Now, how—you might well ask—could a boy raised in the East Neuk of Fife, in a little fishing village so ingrown a boy's cousin might be his uncle as well—how could such a boy know the first thing about silver and gold?

The answer is easier than you might suspect.

The laird and his wife had had a silver wedding anniversary, and a collection was taken up for a special gift from the town. All the small people had given a bit of money they had put aside; the gentry added more. And there was soon enough to hire a silversmith from Edinburgh to make a fine silver centerpiece in the shape of a stag rearing up, surrounded by eight hunting dogs. The dogs looked just like the laird's own pack, including a stiff-legged mastiff with a huge underslung jaw.

The centerpiece had been on display for days in the Crail town hall, near the mercat cross, before the gifting of it. Simon had gone to see it out of curiosity, along with his brothers.

It was the first time that art had ever touched his life.

Touched?

He had been bowled over, knocked about, nearly slain by the beauty of the thing.

After that, fishing meant nothing to him. He wanted to be an artisan. He did not know enough to call it art.

When he got to Edinburgh, a bustle of a place and bigger than twenty Crails laid end to end to end, Simon looked up that same silversmith and begged to become the man's apprentice.

The man would have said no. He had apprentices enough as it was. But some luck was with Simon, for the next day when Simon came around to ask again, two of the lowest apprentices were down with a pox of some kind and had to be sent away. And Simon—who'd been sick with that same pox in his childhood and never again—got to fetch and carry for months on end until by the very virtue of his hard working, the smith offered him a place.

And that is how young Simon Morrison the fisherlad became not-so-young Simon Morrison the silversmith. He was well beyond thirty and not married. He worked so hard, he never had an eye for love, or so it was said by the other lads.

He only had an eye for art.

4.

Now in the great course of things, these two should never have met. Time itself was against them, that greatest divide. A hundred years to be exact.

Besides, Simon would never have gone to America. America was a land of cutthroats and brigands. He did not waste his heart thinking on it, though, in fact, he never wasted his heart on anything but his work.

And though Andrea had once dreamed of Kathmandu and Nepal, she had never fancied Scotland with its "dudes in skirts," as her friend Heidi called them.

But love, though it may take many a circuitous route, somehow manages to get from one end of the map to another.

Always.

5.

Because of the adder rings—a great hit with the Neiman Marcus buyers—Andrea was sent to Scotland by *Vogue* magazine to pose before a ruin of a fourteenth-century castle. The castle, called Dunnottar, commanded a spit of land some two-and-a-half-hours drive along the coast from Edinburgh and had at one point been the hiding place for the Scottish Crown Jewels.

Windy and raw weather did not stop the Dunnottar shoot; in fact, it so speeded things up, the shoot finished early on a Thursday morning. Andrea then had three and a half days to explore the grey stone city of Edinburgh.

She loved the twisty streets and closes, with names like Cowgate and Grassmarket and Lady Wynd, and the antique jewelry shop on a little lane called Thistle.

Edinburgh seemed to be a city of rain and rainbows. A single rainbow over the Greek revival temple on the hill, and a double over the great grey castle.

"If there is such a thing as magic . . ." Andrea found herself whispering aloud, "it's here in this city." For the first time she actually found herself believing in the possibility.

The first two days in Edinburgh went quickly, but she soon tired of tourists who spoke every language except English. She knew she needed some quiet, far away from the Royal Mile and its aggressively Celtic shoppes, and far from the Americanization of Princes Street, the main shopping road, where a McDonald's (without the arches) sat right next to British franchises.

It was then that she discovered a hidden walk that wound around and under the city.

Leith Walk.

Leith had been the old port on the Firth and once a city in its own right, but was now a bustling part of Edinburgh. The old port area after years of decay was now being tarted up, and modernized flats with large *To Let* signs dotted the streets. At first Andrea kept misreading the signs, wondering why toilets were advertised everywhere. Then giggling over her mistake, she went aboard a floating ship restaurant for a quiet lunch alone.

She didn't mean to listen in, but she overheard an elderly English couple near her talking about Leith Walk, which sounded wonderfully off the beaten tourist path.

"Excuse me," she said, leaning over, "I couldn't help hearing you mention Leith Walk. It's not in my book." She pointed to the green Michelin Guide by her plate.

They told her how to find the walk which, they said, snaked under and over parts of Edinburgh along the Leith River.

"Though the locals call it the 'Water of Leith,'" the woman said. "And as you go along, you will often feel as if you had stumbled onto a lost path into faerie."

Andrea was struck by how earnestly she spoke.

"The Walk looks as if it ends up in Dean Village," the English woman added.

"An old grain milling center, that," interrupted her companion. "End of Bell's Brae. Off Queensferry. Solid bridge. Pretty, too." His bristly ginger moustache seemed to strain his words, for they came out crisp and unadorned.

"But do not be fooled, my dear," the woman continued. "It becomes a mere trickle of a path. But it does go on."

"The path . . ." Andrea mused, remembering her Tolkien, "goes ever on . . ."

The English couple laughed and the man said something in a strange tongue.

"I beg your pardon," Andrea said. "I don't speak . . ." She wasn't in fact sure what language he had used.

"I beg *your* pardon," the man said. "Certain you'd know Elvish." His eyes twinkled at her and he no longer seemed so starchy. "I simply wished you a good journey and a safe return."

"Thank you," Andrea said.

She smiled at them as they stood and went out, without, Andrea noticed, leaving any kind of a tip.

6.

Simon was not much of a drinker, certainly not as Scots go. He rarely went out with the lads.

He was a walker, though.

Hill walking when he could get out of the city bustle on holiday.

Town walking when he could not.

He always took his lunch with him and during a work day, he would spend that precious time walking, eating as he went.

Fond of hiking up Calton Hill or Arthur's Seat—both of them affording panoramic views of the city—Simon also liked strolling to the Royal Botanic Garden. There he'd dine amidst the great patches of carefully designed flower beds or, in winter, in the Tropical Palm House, enjoying the moist heat.

Occasionally he would take a sketch book and set off

along the winding Water of Leith walk in the direction of St. Bernard's Well. He passed few people there, unlike his walks up Calton Hill or Arthur's Seat. And he enjoyed the solitude.

The little drawings he did as he sat by the river found their way into his silverwork-intricate twists of foliage, the splay of water over stone, the feathering on the wings of ravens and rooks.

He had begun such drawings as an apprentice, and continued them—with his master's approval—as a journeyman. He perfected them when he became a master silversmith himself.

In time he became famous for them.

In time.

7.

So you think you see the arc of the plot now. They will meet Simon and Andrea—along the Leith Walk.

They will fall in love.

Marry.

And . . .

But you have forgotten that when Andrea takes her first steps along the Leith Walk, heading away from the old port towards Dean's Village and beyond, Simon is already dead some one hundred years earlier. There's not a bit of flesh on those old bones now.

It does present certain intractable problems.

For logic, yes.
Not for love.

8.

It was a lovely early spring afternoon and Simon was grateful to have a half day off. Having had an ugly argument with another of the journeymen over the amount of silver needed for a casting, he wanted some time to walk off his anger.

His anger was with himself more than anyone else, for the other journeyman had been right after all. Simon was not used to making such mistakes.

He was not used to making *any* mistakes.

The master valued Simon too much to argue over half a day. Besides, he knew that with Simon, nothing was ever really lost.

"Go on out, lad," he said. Though Simon was scarcely a lad anymore, the master still thought of him that way. "Walk about and think up some more of yer lovely designs."

Simon decided on following the Leith path, and he walked with a brisk stride that disinvited even a nod from the few people he met along the way.

But by the time he got to St. Bernard's Well—that strange stone neo-Classical folly built by the waterworks over an actual well whose waters were quite the vogue amongst the New Town gentry—the majority of his anger had passed, and he sat down for a bit to sketch, his back against the stone wall.

There was a patch of uncurling ferns near his feet and he loved the sight of the little plants as they unbent their necks. He got the patch down in seven quick lines and then, with three more lines, one fern became a horse's head.

Simon laughed at the conceit. Rather more fanciful than his usual work, but perhaps, he thought, perhaps it was time for *him* to uncurl as well. He was thirty-six years old and half his life gone by. What had happened to the dream that the boy who walked from Crail to Edinburgh had had?

He realized how dreadfully misplaced his anger had been that morning.

As he was thus musing, out of the clear slate of sky there came a crack of thunder.

"By God," Simon cried, and stood up quickly, preparing to run to the sanctuary of the folly. He was a son of fisherfolk, after all, and not about to believe the innocence of that blue sky.

As he turned . . .

9.

Andrea's walk along the Leith River had started quietly enough in bright sunshine. But the weather report on the television that morning had promised scattered sunshine and occasional rain.

"Or was it scattered rain and occasional sunshine?" she murmured. Each of her days in Scotland so far had begun with that same promise from the weather man. Each of those promises had been exactly fulfilled, Scottish weather being charmingly predictable.

The scattering began with a bit of spitting, not enough rain to be worried about, only enough to be annoying.

Andrea had no idea where the next exit from the Leith Walk might be, and there was no way she was going to climb over the fence, go through that little woods, and then scale the stone wall she could almost make out, just to get away from a spatter. She'd been a mountain hiker too long to worry about such things.

Besides, she thought—jamming her pretty blue Scottish tam on her head and tucking her hair under it—in her khaki pants and Aran sweater she was more than ready for a wee bit of rain. In fact she positively welcomed it.

But the little rain suddenly turned into a downpour.

Luckily that was when she spotted the stone temple ahead. Racing for it, she got in the lee of the wall before the major flood opened up overhead.

Mounting the steps two at a time, she thought she was safe when, without warning, a bolt of lightning struck a little spire on the top of the temple's roof, traveled down a wire, and leaped over to the metal ornament on her tam.

She did not so much feel the shock as smell it, a kind

of sharpness in the nose and on the tongue. Her skin prickled, the little hairs rising up on her arms. Then she sank into unconsciousness, falling over the side of the wall and onto the slippery grass below.

10.

A bolt from the blue, you are thinking.

How corny.

The sky *was* actually blue at the moment, except for patches of clouds scudding backwards, in an effort to escape time.

Andrea's eyelids fluttered open.

She sighed.

The first thing she saw was the face of a very concerned youngish man staring down at her.

The second thing she saw was that his eyes were the same bleached blue as the sky over them.

Then she noticed the ginger eyebrows and the cheekbones sharp enough to cut cheese with.

"Am I dead?" Andrea whispered. "Are you an angel?"

Corny, yes.

But most lives are as filled with corn as a Kansas field.

Or—if you prefer—a cornfield in east Fife.

Different kinds of corn, of course.

Different kinds of lives.

11.

One minute Simon had been sitting quietly drawing. The next minute he heard the crack of thunder, and after that a body came hurtling over the side of the stone wall and sprawled face up at his feet.

For a moment Simon thought it was a boy. The tam and the pants confused him. But once he'd looked carefully—at the face with its lambent skin, at the long black curls spilling out of the tam, at the soft swell of breast beneath the woolen jumper—he knew it was no boy.

Then the fallen girl's eyes opened. They were almost purple, enormous, lovely.

"Am I dead?" she asked. "Are you an angel?"

"Och, lass, I'm a silversmith. And how could ye have died from that wee jump?" he asked.

"I mean from the lightning," she said.

He glanced up, worried. After all—there *had* been thunder. But the grey clouds had sped away.

Glancing down, he said, "No lightning, lass. I think ye swooned and fell over the wall."

"I'm not the swooning type," she said.

"Then what type are ye?"

He meant nothing bad by the question, but she looked confused. Then she tried to sit up and seemed to be having difficulty doing it. So Simon put a hand to her back to help her up. And though he'd never put an arm around a woman before without being related to her, this seemed so natural that he did not give it another thought.

However, it was then that he realized she was not the *young* lass he'd taken her for. There were a few strands of silver in her hair, tangling through the curls. He imagined taking that silver and weaving it into a pattern on a bracelet.

As his master knew, nothing with Simon was ever lost.

12.

She saw his sketches, she pulled a small notebook from a back pocket of her trousers and showed him hers. They spoke of silver and gold and the intricacies of cloisonné. They talked of working with electrum and foil and plating. They compared the virtues of enameling and embossing.

They did not speak of love.

It was too soon.

And soon it was too late.

Somewhere a minute or an hour or a day or a week later, they figured out the difference in time.

"You're an old man when I am born," she mused.

"I am dead when you are born," he said.

But time has a way of correcting itself. Of making sense of nonsense.

And one minute or an hour or a day or a week later, Andrea turned a corner of a street off Grassmarket—dressed now of course as a young woman should—and she went in one step from streetcars to Subarus.

"Simon!" she cried, turning back.

But Simon and his century were gone.

13.

Andrea returned home but she didn't feel at home. The sky over Chappaqua had a dirty, smudged look. The air reeked. She could not bear the billboards along the highway nor the myriad choices of toilet cleansers and bath soaps at the super market.

She shut off her TV and sold her fax. She went shopping for long skirts and shirtwaists in secondhand shops.

She told her customers that she had a great deal of back work to do and gave them the names of several other jewelers they might patronize instead.

She said goodbye to her three friends.

"I'm thinking of moving to Scotland," she told them. She did not tell them where.

Or when.

Then she sold her parents' house, took the money in a banker's check, bought a ticket on Icelandair, and flew with a small suitcase of secondhand clothes to Scotland.

The Royal Bank of Scotland was more than happy to open an account for her, and she rented a small flat in Leith.

Then she set to work. Not as a silversmith, not as a jewelry maker. She became a researcher, haunting the

Edinburgh churches to see if she could find where Simon had been buried. To see if there was some mention of him in the town rolls.

Her search took her the better part of a year, but she had time.

The rest of my life if needed, she thought. Her parents' house had brought in a great deal of money. It was not money that worried her. It was the rest of Simon's life she was afraid of.

Once she'd been through every cemetery in the city she was at a loss, until she remembered that Simon had once spoken of being an East Neuk lad. On a whim she went by bus out to Crail, the little fishing village Simon had mentioned.

It was a pearl of a village with a mercat cross topped by a unicorn in the center of the upper town. The tolbooth was a tiered tower with a graceful belfry. When she went along the shop row, passing a bakery and a butcher's, she was stopped by a glass-fronted jewelry store. It sold both new pieces—rather simple and not terribly interesting—and antique ware. Glancing up at the sign over the lintel, she was stunned.

MORRISONS
JEWELRY SINCE 1878

Trembling, she went in.

14.

You've guessed it now.

How the story ends.

But you are wrong again.

Andrea does not find Simon, for he is long gone and no amount of standing about in electrical storms can bring her back again in time.

Who she finds is the great-great-grandson of Simon Morrison, who is also named Simon.

And that Simon, on hearing the name Andrea Crow, immediately gives her a job as a jewelry maker in the shop because it has been a family legend—accompanied by a notarized document—that some time in the new century such a young woman would come. Black curls, violet eyes, and a master jeweler's skill.

In his early thirties, this Simon looks nothing like old Simon. He has a roundness to his face and a sunny disposition. He does not so much make jewelry as sell what others make.

After half a year, he proposes and Andrea accepts and they marry, though Andrea explains that some part of her will always belong to old Simon.

This young Simon understands. It is, after all, part of the family tradition. Scots are big on lost causes.

Andrea's designs become popular in Scotland and then England and then the Continent. Neiman Marcus rediscovers her work. She and Simon have three children.

And in time they fall in love.

In time.

DARK SEED, DARK STONE

They have already started on Father's stone, right after the blowing of the horns. The first cut by Painted Oengus was for the broken spear because Father was the clan's greatest warrior. He was called Bridei's Hound because he had so often run before the king. And Bridei's Shield, because he put his body over the king's when the spears were the thickest.

A great warrior, and brother-in-law to the king, but not, alas, great enough. He had a mere man's skin after all, and a Northumbrian's knife pierced it easily. Such a small slice for life to have leaked out.

After we watch Painted Oengus set his chisel to the stone, we come here to lay out Father's body for burial. I fasten his cloak around his shoulders with his best brooch, the one Mother had made for him to honor his first battle. I set my long finger over the wound in his neck. It covers the wound completely. Stepmother shouts at me and I take my hand away. But not before I feel how small Father's death is.

I walk away from the corpse table then, because Stepmother shouts and because I cannot stand to see her weeping over Father as if she loved him. She married him for status alone after my mother—Bridei's sister—died. But Stepmother never showed him softness while he lived. It shames us all how she carries on now, anointing his cold flesh with her hot tears. I think she worries that no one will ask for her in marriage once the mourning year is over, or that Bridei will not allow it, wishing her to mourn Father for the rest of her life. She has not shown herself fertile and her tongue is sharp enough to cut off her lips. Who would marry a barren woman, no matter how tall she is, how beautiful.

I go from the hall where his body lies and find my way to the byre to be with the cows, who are at least warm and smell of the earth, not flower scents ground in a mortar and warmed behind a woman's ears.

Cattle cannot cry falsely. Indeed, they cannot cry at all. Nor can they rail at me. I like that.

No one bothers me here, in the round stone byre. I am, after all, only a third daughter of a dead wife of a dead warrior. I am not beautiful like my sister Alba of the White Arms, who looks like our mother. I am not a fine weaver like my sister Golden Eithni of the Upright Loom, who has our mother's skills. Both of them are already married, and to warriors nearly as great as Father had been.

Me—I am no one. Bryony, the Dark Seed. I am short and have Father's black hair and dark skin, his broad hands and large feet. Although it is true I have his knowledge of the land and a fierce heart, those are not a woman's skills. I am already thirteen and no one has spoken for me yet.

I doubt any will.

Really, cows are better company than men.

But I do not want to stay with the cows, whose conversation is so limited. I head back to where Painted Oengus is at work on the next carving, using as his guide the pictures tattooed on his arms, his ankles, his chest. I know that next he will chisel out a sword, then a horse or a chariot, Father's honors as a warrior.

There will likely be a salmon as well. We are the Salmon people, my father's mother having come from among the tribes of the Great Silver River where salmon were once so thick, one could cross to the far side by walking on their backs. Or so she used to tell me.

And there will be other Signs—whatever Bridei instructs. He is king and Father was his Hound and his Shield after all.

Even Stepmother cannot override Bridei's wishes. Sometimes I wish that I could be king. But I am a girl. My wishes should be for a husband and children, for yellow corn, fat cows, a tight loom—as my sisters do not hesitate to remind me.

Bridei had sent for Painted Oengus all the way from the Black Firth to make Father's stone, and he had begun the work at once. Now he is kneeling before the stone, holding his great chisel and pounding it with a wooden hammer. The one finished picture—of the broken spear—stands out boldly. I think he has rubbed it with red clay to bring out the lines. Father's blood had dried to that color. I know it well. I washed the wound with my tears first, water after.

The second carving—a hound with its hair streaming behind—has already been outlined on the stone. Painted Oengus is a careful carver, but he is quick, too. The best of all The People, so Eithni says.

I stand behind him, peering over his shoulder. Since Stepmother is not here to yell at me, no one will stop me from watching.

Painted Oengus is a short man, though no shorter than Father. His hair—the color of the flaming sunset skies—is shot through with strands of white. He hums as he works. It is not a tune I know. But then Painted Oengus comes from afar. His bards would not be our bards.

I dare a question. "Will there be a mirror?" A mirror would mean that my stepmother has paid for the stone. Mirrors are women's signs. As are combs.

He grunts, which is not an answer.

Just then Bridei is at my shoulder. "There will be no mirror, Bryony," he tells me. "I have paid for the stone and the carver." He strikes his chest for emphasis. "This stone is the clan's doing, not the outland wife's. Your father will have a warrior's signs because he was my brother-in-law and a man. In life and in death."

I nod, unable to speak, the word *death* filling my head.

"Now go home and help with the mourning feast or that woman will have a fit and call down her dark gods upon us." He says *that woman* with much bitterness. "And that will dishonor my Shield."

Well, he is the king and must be obeyed. In peace as well as in war. Unlike some clans over the sea I have heard of who are ruled in peace by Speakers and only in war follow their king.

So I go home to the long house, the house that was once my Father's and is no more.

When I arrive, Stepmother screams at me that I have failed to get the fire started or fetch in the water. Of course, we both know that there are servants to do all this, and they have *not* failed. The fire is roaring in the hearth. In the wooden bucket, water brims to the top. The table is already set with platters piled high with slabs of venison and boar. There is ale in the mugs. Salads of sorrel nestle in bowls, as well as boiled scurvy grass and nuts finely cracked, and dried berries and plums from last year's fruiting.

But Stepmother needs to take out her worry in anger, and as I am Father's only child still at home, I am convenient.

Her voice is so loud, it carries throughout the settlement, and she shames us both. The guests already starting across the grass to our house hear her shrilling. I can see through the open door the pain and embarrassment on their faces.

I run outside past the guests, back to the byre again, knowing I will not starve with cow's milk to hand. And I can sleep there, warmed by cow's breath and my father's second-best cloak, which I have hidden in a rock safe for just such a purpose. It is not my first time sleeping away from my stepmother's house. It will not be my last.

My sister Alba finds me.

"Bryony," she says, "do not shame us more by absenting yourself from the feast." She puts her arms about me. I love the familiar smell of breast milk and slightly damp woolen cloth. Alba has a new baby, another girl, a sweet little thing named Ionia. But still I pull away from her and shake my head.

"I hate our stepmother. I will not go back."

"She is nothing, that one," Alba continues. We can both still hear Stepmother. "She is less than nothing. A woman with an empty womb and no future. Soon sent back to her own people with only her jewels, if the gods are merciful."

I nod. Of course Alba is right. But still I hesitate.

"Come back to the feast, Bryony," she says. "For Father. For his honor." She puts her small white hand on my broader, darker hand.

"For Father," I whisper, and leave the cows.

Even Stepmother cannot spoil the feast, though she tries. She complains about me, about Father who left her, about the rough lives of The People compared to her own clan, about the weather and the wind and the little black bugs that bite. It is her way and nobody but me really listens anymore.

There is plenty to eat, which honors Father. Alba and Eithni contribute breads and small cakes. Our cousins—Father's sisters' families—have slaughtered a cow, and not an old one, either.

Every warrior who has fought by Father's side brings a gift: cloth, combs, silver torques and chains and pins. We will choose the best to bury with him, the rest will reside in my stepmother's coffers.

Until she leaves.

I keep that thought to myself, warming my cold heart with it. *Until she leaves.*

The Speaker has made a prayer for Father's passage

and the bard sings a new song—"Song of the Hound and Shield" he calls it.

Some of the words I will never forget:

Take our Hound to the bright lands,
Let him course through sweet meadows,
Oh, let him follow the deer.

The men cheer at each verse. The women call out Father's name and say his virtues. And Bridei makes toast after toast. Bridei and his children have brought along enough strong ale to drown the entire clan.

Everybody drinks, Stepmother most of all, for she is trying to keep up with Bridei, to show that she is her husband's equal and not to be sent back like a useless slave. But at last she collapses, her head on the table.

Bridei winks at me and signals his children to carry her off to bed.

I smile back at him. But I am worried, too. Without Father to be Bridei's Shield—for he has no sons and no more brothers—who will guard him in the next fight?

At last the guests go, at least those who are still standing. The rest will snore away the night at our long table. I cannot ask the servants to clean up till morning. That would bring dishonor to those who have feasted Father. They have to be left to their dreams.

I go outside for some fresh air.

The stars above are many but there is no moon. I walk past the byre, past the houses of the clan. Climbing up the stairs to the great walls of the settlement, I adjust the shawl on my shoulders, pinning it tight against the chill with my mother's silver-and-red enamel brooch.

There are no guards on the wall this night. I have left them sleeping at our table.

As I walk, I pray silently: *Let* me *be Bridei's Shield now that Father is gone. Let* me *guard his back.*

The gods do not answer. I am not a Speaker, after all. Only Speakers get to talk to the gods and expect an answer. Of course, our Speaker would warn me, had he heard me, that the gods' answers are not always what we wish. But I do not care and this time say my prayer aloud. "Let me take Father's place as Bridei's Shield."

For a long time after I stand on the wall, gazing out across the rolling land. Far away, on the other side of the long meres, are our enemies, the Northumbrians. Father's killers.

I think about them, the dark warriors with their iron hats. I think about them and hate them so fiercely, there is a white-hot flame searing beneath my breastbone.

Suddenly a strange light streaks across the sky, making a sound like a thousand cicadas. I tremble and fall to my knees, for when a star travels from one side of the world to the other, it is a sign from the gods. It means a journey of greatness.

Will it be my journey? I wonder. Or does it signify Father's trip to the underworld?

When I look down again at the rolling land, I see someone running along the ridge. A man. It is too dark to see if he is one among many, but he is not wearing an iron hat. He is not sneaking as do Northumbrians. He is running tall, like one of The People.

I hurry down from the wall and go straight to the king's house, knocking frantically at the door.

Bridei himself opens it.

"There is a man," I say. "Coming. Coming . . ." I cannot get it out all at once, for I am almost out of breath. "No guards . . . on the wall . . . But I . . . I saw only . . . one!" I draw in an enormous breath and finish with a burst, "One running man on the ridge!"

Bridei does not smile. He reaches for his great spear that stands at the door, and shouts back to his household. "Get the men up!" He turns to me. "It would be just like the Southerners to attack at night. And when we are feasting our dead. They have no honor." He hefted his spear. "Just *one* you say?"

"I could see no others."

He hands me a knife. "Are you your father's daughter?"

I nod. I have gutted deer and boar. I guess I can gut a man.

Bridei shouts again. I hear people stirring in the darkness behind him. Then he looks at me.

"Wake your sisters' husbands and the rest."

"And the guards sleeping at our table?" I ask.

He reaches a hand out to tousle my hair. "Throw water on them if necessary. The gods will understand. There will be no dishonor in it."

I run off to do his bidding.

My sisters' husbands are easy to wake. They get up from their pallets and immediately take spears and bows, though at night a bow is almost useless. Still, morning will be on us soon.

The men asleep at our house are more difficult. I shout but no one stirs. I do not touch them. They are men and I am an unmarried girl.

There is little water left in the bucket and no time to get more. I pour good ale on two of them and leave them to wake the rest. Then I hurry back to see Bridei and his household guards rushing out of the gate.

Painted Oengus, who has slept in the king's house, stands looking at them.

"Why are you not off fighting with them?" I ask.

"Not my fight," he says in his grunt voice. "I be no fighter."

"You carry a spear," I tell him with passion, nodding at his left hand. I show him my knife.

He throws back his head and laughs loudly. "Must have protection from wild beast. They do not know I be great carver." He hits his chest with the flat of his hand.

I am furious. "Do not laugh at me. Not when we are about to fight for our clan."

Painted Oengus stops laughing, though there is still a smile on his face. "Little fierce one," he says, "your clansmen do not go to fight. They go to greet runner. He be alone, streaking across ridge like great star."

I gasp. He has used the same words as I. Is it another sign? I do not know how to ask that question, so I ask another: "Who is it?"

"How to know from here?" He puts out a hand. "Come."

I take his hand. It is as big as Father's.

We walk outside the gates, but I am careful to keep my knife at the ready.

"My father was Bridei's Shield," I tell Oengus.

"Yes."

"I must be his Shield now."

He looks down at me and smiles again. "Then Bridei be well kept."

Our men have surrounded the running man, who is tall and straight and has hair as dark as mine tied back with a leather thong. His trews are so filthy, I am not able to see the pattern of his clan. His chest is bare and there is much thick hair curling there. A silver crossbar hanging from a silver chain nestles in that hair.

Bridei's guards take him by the arm and the running man does not pull away. Instead he slaps himself on the chest, right over the silver crossbar, with his free hand and speaks what must have been his name, but the word is strange in my ears, sounding like water over stone. Then he spies Painted Oengus, and says something more.

Painted Oengus answers. When he speaks the running man's tongue, his voice does not grunt, which makes me wonder.

The guards bring the man toward Bridei. Gripping my knife, I edge forward.

Close up, the running man has strange eyes, one blue, one brown. Perhaps he is a Speaker. Perhaps he has been sent by the gods.

But, I wonder, *are they our gods—or his?*

He breaks free of the guards and runs toward Bridei. I race before him and bring up my knife.

But in one swift movement, he has the knife from my hand, my hand in his grip. He kneels before Bridei, speaking in his watery tongue. My hand in his feels as if it is in the cleft of a tree. I cannot move the fingers nor take the hand away. I have but one choice. I turn under him, nearly breaking my hand off at the wrist, and throw myself upon his back. I angle my free arm around his neck.

"Bridei," I cry out, "I am your Shield now. Strike this man while you can!" Though we all know that to strike the man, the spear will have to go through me first. But I am ready. I, Bryony, the Dark Seed.

Painted Oengus comes forward, both hands stretched before him. "Do not strike, oh King. This man known to me. He be king's son. He asks sanctuary . . ." I do not move. Nor does anyone else. Even the stars above us, I believe, are still.

Then the Speaker comes forward. He stands at the running man's head. "Tell us again your name." He slaps his own chest with the question. "Name?"

The running man does not move, does not try to stand with me on his back, but says clearly, "Eanfrid."

And this time I hear it complete. It runs through my head the way the star ran across the sky. "Eanfrid."

His back is cold beneath me. I feel the rumble of his voice through my bones. He speaks longer now, and again Painted Oengus tells us his words.

"I am Eanfrid, oldest of Ethelfrid's sons. Our kinsman has killed our father and stolen his crown. Let me live here, under your protection and name, till I can take back what is mine."

Bridei listens, his hand tangling in his beard.

My wrist is ready to break, but still I do not move.

Then Bridei speaks. "Bryony, climb down. I do not need your death. I want your life. But for your courage, I will give you a boon. Only ask it and it is yours."

I have nothing to ask, except that my Father be returned to me, and this Bridei cannot do. Or that Stepmother be sent away at once. But to ask that would not be honorable. Besides, it will be done in time. I need not waste my boon on her.

Bridei is still speaking. "This man, Eanfrid, will stay. Though the Northumbrians have no honor, killing their own kings, we will treat this Eanfrid as if he is a man of The People once he has learned our ways. Then will he have honor." I see he has difficulty saying this. The newness of it makes him uncomfortable.

Painted Oengus tells Eanfrid what Bridei has said and Eanfrid lets go of my hand. I fall off his back, making a sound like a cow in labor. He moves to help me up and I shrug away his hand. His two-colored eyes look soft and hurt. He tries a smile. His teeth are very white and even. I see he is younger than I first thought. Not long from his boyhood.

Then Alba's husband puts me behind him, as if I need hiding. I, who have just thrown myself on an enemy's back. He means well, but he only sees me as a younger sister to his wife, and forgets that I am my Father's daughter.

I hold my wrist where the pain is greatest and walk back to the hall of mourning while the others go on to Bridei's house to celebrate the newest member of our clan. They will feast him as if he is newborn. Both men and women.

In the hall of mourning, I kneel before the corpse, who is only now beginning to stink. "Father," I say, "they have traded a runner for a warrior. A Northumbrian for a man of The People."

He gives no answer, nor do I expect any.

My wrist is aching, but my heart is aching more. Things are changing and I do not like them to change.

"Father," I say, putting a hand on the cold, now-unfamiliar flesh, "tell me what to do."

I hear a rumble, like words coming from a cave. The hall suddenly seems full of mist. I cannot see. My wrist hurts. I turn toward the door, fearing fire.

But the words do not come from the door; they come from behind me. From Father. It is not possible but it is true. Father's ghost speaks to me, his voice sounding as if it comes from the bottom of our settlement's great well.

"Be Bridei's Shield," he says. "Ask your boon from Bridei. Have him give you the Northumbrian's head and hands to send back to the new king of his land."

I fall down onto my sore wrist. My head hits the ground. I bite my tongue almost in two. There are stars over me, shooting along the rooftrees of the hall.

Eithni finds me lying outstretched before Father's corpse. I am on my back, weeping.

She does not ask. She thinks she knows what has happened.

She does not.

With her help, I rise and she makes me drink fresh water from a cup. My mouth is full of blood. I spit it out and then we go to Bridei's house. They are still raising glasses of ale to the new man. He is swathed like a baby. Each woman of The People holds him for a moment to her breast.

I walk in. My wrist hurts, my head hurts, my tongue hurts, and I no longer care.

"Bridei," I say thickly, "I have come to claim that boon."

The man, Eanfrid, hears the strange power in my voice. For a moment there is fear in his eyes, then hardness. He will be brave whatever I ask.

I walk up to him and put my sore hand on his shoulder. "Give me this man."

"He is yours," Bridei says casually, but there is a slyness in his eyes. Honor demands he honor my request. He thinks he knows what I want.

He does not.

I tell him. "Give me this man as husband. Two royal lines will be wed that way. I and all my children will thus be your Shield forever."

Bridei's mouth gets small and round. He thinks a long time. He does not like change any more than I. He has already made one change this night. Now I have asked for another. He thinks about the Northumbrians who have killed one king. He thinks how easily they would kill another.

Beneath my hand Eanfrid's flesh is warm. He does not know what we are speaking of, but he knows. I can feel his knowledge and his strength. It takes courage to run from all you know and to seek sanctuary with your enemies. It takes courage and will. He must be a stronger man than his father. I am counting on this.

At last Bridei speaks. "Your advice is as good as your Father's."

I remember the hollow voice speaking to me of death. The old way.

"Better," I say, and smile. Once for Bridei to whom I owe honor, once to Father to whom I owe memory, and once to my husband to whom I owe love.

Historical note: Eanfrid was the oldest of the three sons of Ethelfrid, King of Bernica, the northernmost of the English kingdoms, i.e., Northumbria. When Ethelfrid was defeated by his cousin Edwin in 617, his sons were sent into exile along with many other young nobles until Edwin's death in 633. There the boys grew up among the Picts and Scots. All three of the brothers were converted to Christianity and baptized during their exiles. According to one source, Eanfrid "took the politically important step of marrying into the Pictish royal family. We do not know the name of his wife, but . . . she bore him a son, Talorgan, who was to become King of the Pict . . ." Years later, in 685, under a different Bridei (son of Bili), the Picts would slaughter the Northumbrian enemy at the Battle of Nechtansmere and kill the Northumbrian king.

DRAGONFIELD

There is a spit of land near the farthest shores of the farthest islands. It is known as Dragonfield. Once dragons dwelt on the isles in great herds, feeding on the dry brush and fueling their flames with the carcasses of small animals and migratory birds. There are no dragons there now, though the nearer islands are scored with long furrows as though giant claws had been at work, and the land is fertile from the bones of the buried behemoths. Yet though the last of the great worms perished long before living memory, there is a tale still told by the isles' farmers and fisherfolk about that last dragon.

His name in the old tongue was Aredd and his color a dull red. It was not the red of hollyberry or the red of the wild flowering trillium, but the red of a man's lifeblood spilled out upon the sand. Aredd's tail was long and sinewy, his body longer still. Great mountains rose upon his back. His eyes were black, and when he was angry, looked as empty as the painted eyes of a shroud, but when he was calculating, they shone with a false jeweled light. His jaws were a furnace that could roast a whole bull. And when he roared, he could be heard like distant thunder throughout the archipelago.

Aredd was the last of his kind and untaught in the riddle lore of dragons. He was but fierceness and fire, for he had hatched late from the brood. His brothers and sisters were all gone, slain in the famous Dragon Wars when even young dragons were spitted by warriors who had gone past fearing. But the egg that had housed Aredd had lain buried in the sand of Dragonfield years past the carnage, uncovered at last by an unnaturally high tide. And when he hatched, no one had remarked it. So the young worm had stretched and cracked the shell and emerged nose first in the sand.

At the beginning he looked like any large lizard, for he had not yet shed his eggskin, which was lumpy and whitish, like clotted cream. But he grew fast, as dragons will, and before the week was out he was the size of a small pony and his eggskin had sloughed off. He had, of course, singed and eaten the skin and so developed a taste for crackling. A small black-snouted island pig was his next meal, then a family of shagged cormorants flying island to island on their long migration south.

And still no one remarked him, for it was the time of great harvests brought about by the fertilization of the rich high tides, and everyone was needed in the fields: old men and women, mothers with their babes tied to their backs, ardent lovers who might have slipped off to the Jar isle to tryst. Even the young fishermen did not dare to go down to the bay and cast off while daylight bathed the plants and vines. They gave up their nets and lines for a full two weeks to help with the "stripping," as the harvest was called then. And by night, of course, the villagers were much too weary to sail by moonlight to the spit.

Another week, then, and Aredd was a dull red, could trickle smoke rings through his nostrils, and had grown to the size of a bull. His wings, still crumpled and weak, lay untested along his sides, but his foreclaws, which had been as brittle as shells at birth, were now as hard as golden oak. He had sharpened them against the beach boulders, leaving scratches as deep as worm runnels. At night he dreamed of blood.

The tale of Aredd's end, as it is told in the farthest islands, is also the tale of a maiden once called Tansy after the herb of healing, but was later known as Areddiana, daughter of the dragon. Of course it is a tale with a hero. That is why there are dragons, after all: to call forth heroes. But he was a hero in spite of himself and because of Tansy. The story goes thus:

There were three daughters of a healer who lived on the northern shore of Medd, the largest isle of the archipelago. Although they had proper names, after the older gods, they were always called by their herbal names.

Rosemary, the eldest, was a weaver. Her face was plain but honest, a face that would wear well with time. Her skin was dark as if she spent her days out in the sun, though, in truth, she preferred the cottage's cold dirt floors and warm hearth. Her lips were full but she kept them thin. She buffed the calluses on her hands to make them shine. She had her mother's gray eyes and her passion for work, and it annoyed her that others did not.

Sage was the beauty, but slightly simple. She was as golden as Rosemary was brown, and brushed her light-filled hair a full hundred strokes daily. She worked when told to, but otherwise preferred to stare out the window at the sea. She was waiting, she said, for her own true love. She had even put it in rhyme.

Glorious, glorious, over the sea,
My own true love will come for me.

She repeated it so often that they all believed it to be true.

Tansy was no special color at all; rather she seemed to blend in with her surroundings, sparkling by a stream, golden in the sunny meadows, mouse brown within the house. She was the one who was a trouble to her mother: early walking and always picking apart things that had been knit up with great care just to see what made them work. So she was named after the herb that helped women in their times of trouble. Tansy. It was hoped that she would grow into her name.

"Where is that girl?" May-Ma cried.

Her husband, crushing leaves for a poultice, knew without asking which girl she meant. Only with Tansy did May-Ma's voice take on an accusatory tone.

"I haven't seen her for several hours, May-Ma," said Rosemary from the loom comer. She did not even look up but concentrated on the market cloth she was weaving.

"That Tansy. She is late again for her chores. Probably dreaming somewhere. Or eating some new and strange concoction." May-Ma's hands moved on the bread dough as if preparing to beat a recalcitrant child. "Someday, mind you, someday she will eat herself past your help, Da."

The man smiled to himself. Never would he let such a thing happen to his Tansy. She had knowledge, precious and god-given, and nothing she made was past his talents for healing. Besides, she seemed to know instinctively how far to taste, how far to test, and she had a high tolerance for pain.

"Mind you," May-Ma went on, pounding the dough into submission, "Now, mind you, I'm not saying she doesn't have a Gift. But Gift or no, she has chores to do." Her endless repetitions had begun with the birth of her first child and had increased with each addition to the family until now, three live children later (she never mentioned the three little boys buried under rough stones at the edge of the garden), she repeated herself endlessly. "Mind you, a Gift is no excuse."

"I'm minding, May-Ma," said her husband, wiping his hands on his apron. He kissed her tenderly on the head as if to staunch the flow of words, but still they bled out.

"If she would remember her chores as well as she remembers dreams," May-Ma went on, "As well as she remembers the seven herbs of binding, the three parts to setting a broken limb, the . . ."

"I'm going, May-Ma," whispered her husband into the flood, and left.

He went outside and down a gentle path winding towards the river, guessing that on such a day Tansy would be picking cress.

The last turn opened onto the river and never failed to surprise him with joy. The river was an old one, its bends broad as it flooded into the great sea. Here and there the water had cut through soft rock to make islets that could be reached by pole boat or, in the winter, by walking across the thick ice. This turning, green down to the river's edge, was full of cress and reeds and even wild rice carried from the Eastern lands by migrating birds.

"Tansy," he called softly, warning her of his coming.

A gull screamed back at him. He dropped his eyes to the hatchmarked tracks of shorebirds in the mud, waited a moment to give her time to answer, and then when none came, called again. "Tansy. Child."

"Da, Da, here!" It was the voice of a young woman, breathless yet throaty, that called back. "And see what I have found. I do not know what it is."

The reeds parted and she stepped onto the grass. Her skirts were kilted up, bunched at her waist. Even so they were damp and muddy. Her slim legs were coated with a green slime and there was a smear of that same muck along her nose and across her brow where she had obviously wiped away sweat or a troublesome insect. She held up a sheaf of red grassy weeds, the tops tipped with pink florets. Heedless of the blisters on her fingers, she gripped the stalk.

"What is it?" she asked. "It hurts something fierce, but I've never seen it before. I thought you might know."

"Drop it. Drop it at once, child. Where are your mitts?"

At his cry, she let the stalk go and it landed in the water, spinning around and around in a small eddy, a spiral of smoke uncurling from the blossoms.

He plucked her hand toward him and reached into his belt bag. Taking out a cloth-wrapped packet of fresh aloe leaves, he broke one leaf in two and squeezed out the healing oils onto her hands. Soon the redness around the blisters on her fingers was gone, though the blisters remained like a chain of tiny seed pearls.

"Now will you tell me what it is?" she asked, grinning up at him despite what he knew to be a terribly painful burn. There was a bit of mischief in her smile too, which kept him from scolding her further about her gloves.

"I have never seen it before, only heard of it. I thought it but a tale. It is called fireweed or flamewort. You can guess why. The little blisters on the hand are in the old rhyme. It grows only where a great dragon lives or so the spellbook says:

Leaves of blood and sores of pearl,
In the sea, a smoky swirl,
Use it for your greatest need,
Dragon's Bane and fireweed.

"They used it somehow in the dragon wars. But child, look at your hands!"

She looked down for the first time and caught her breath as she saw the tiny, pearly sores. "One, two, three . . . why there must be fifteen blisters here," she said, fascinated. "Sores of pearl indeed. But what is its use?"

Her father shook his head and wrapped the aloe carefully. "I cannot imagine, since the sting of it is so fierce. And if the note about it be true, it will burn for near an hour once the florets open, burn with a hot steady flame that cannot be put out. Then it will crumble all at once into red ash. So you leave it there, steaming on the water and come home with me. There is *no use* for dragon's bane, for there are no more dragons."

The fireweed had already lost its color in the river, graying out, but still it sent up a curl of blue-white steam. Tansy found a stick and pushed it towards the stalk and where she touched, the weed flared up again a bright red. When she pulled back the stick, the color of the weed faded as quickly as a blush. The stick burned down towards Tansy's fingers and she dropped it into the river where it turned to ash and floated away.

"Dragon's bane," she whispered. "And I wonder why." She neglected to mention to her father that there was a large patch of the weed growing, hidden, in the reeds.

"Such questions will not win you favor at home," her father said, taking her unblistered hand in his. "Especially not with your dear May-Ma ready to do your chores. She will chide you a dozen times over for the same thing if we do not hurry home."

"My chores!" Tansy cried. Then she shrugged and looked at her father with wise eyes. "Even if I were home to do them, I would hear of it again and again. Poor May-Ma, she speaks to herself for none of the rest of us really talks to her." She pulled away from him and was gone up the path as if arrowshot.

He chuckled aloud and walked to the water's edge to pick some fresh peppermint and sweet woodruff for teas. The river's slow meandering was still noisy enough that he did not hear the strange chuffing sound of heavy new wings above him. It was only when the swollen shadow darkened the ground that he looked up and into the belly of a beast he had thought long extinct. He was so surprised; he did not have time to cry out or to bless himself before dying. The flames that killed him were neither long nor especially hot, but fear and loathing added their toll. The healer was dead before his body touched earth. He never felt the stab of the golden claws as the dragon carried him back to its home on the far spit of land.

Only the singed open herb bag, its contents scattered on the path, bore testimony to the event.

They did not look for him until near dark. And then, in the dark, with only their small tapers for light, they missed the burned herb sack. It was morning before they found it and Sage had run off to their closest neighbors for help.

What help could be given? The healer was gone, snatched from the good earth he had so long tended. They could not explain the singed sack, and so did not try. They concentrated instead on his missing body. Perhaps he had fallen, one man suggested, into the river. Since he was not a fisherman, he could not swim. They expected his body to fetch up against an island shore within a few days. Such a thing had happened to men before. The fisherfolk knew where to look. And that was all the comfort the villagers had to lend. It was harvest, after all, and they could spare only the oldest women to weep and prepare funeral pies.

"And what kind of funeral is it?" May-Ma asked repeatedly. "Without a body, what kind of burial? He will be back. Back to laugh at our preparations. I know it. I know it here." She touched her breast and looked out to the garden's edge and the large, newly-cut stone overshadowing the three smaller ones. "He will be back."

But she was the only one to hold out such hope, and to no one's surprise but May-Ma's, the healer did not return. The priest marked his passing with the appropriate signs and psalms, then returned to help with the harvest. The girls wept quietly: Rosemary by her loom, dampening the cloth; Sage by the window, gazing off down the path; Tansy alone in the woods. May-Ma sobbed her hopes noisily and the villagers, as befitting their long friendship with the healer, spoke of his Gift with reverence. It did not bring him back.

The healer's disappearance became a small mystery in a land used to small mysteries until after the harvest was in. And then Tam-the-Carpenter's finest draft horse was stolen. A week and a half later, two prize ewes were taken from Mother Comfy's fold. And almost two weeks after that, the latest of the cooper's twelve children disappeared from its cradle in the meadow when the others had left it for just a moment to go and pick wild trillium in the dell. A great fear descended upon the village then. They spoke of ravening beasts, of blood-crazed goblins, of a mad changeling beast-man roaming the woods, and looked at one another with suspicion. The priest ranted of retribution and world's end. But none of them considered dragons, for, as they knew full well, the last of the great worms had been killed in the dragon wars. And while none had actually seen a goblin or a beast-man, and while there had not been wild animals larger than a goldskin fox in the woods for twice two hundred years, still such creatures seemed likelier than dragons. Dragons, they knew with absolute and necessary conviction, were no more.

It was a fisherman who saw Aredd and lived to tell of it. In a passion one early morning, he had gone over the side of his boat to untangle a line. It was a fine line, spun out over the long winter by his wife, and he was not about to lose it, for the mark of its spinning was still on his wife's forefinger and thumb. The line was down a great ways underwater and he had scarcely breath enough to work it free of a black root. But after three dives he had worked it loose and was surfacing again when he saw the bright water above him suddenly darken. He knew water too well to explain it, but held his breath longer and slowed his ascent until the darkness had passed by. Lucky it was, for when he broke through the foam, the giant body was gone past, its claws empty. All the fisherman saw clearly through water-filmed eyes was the great rudder of its red tail. He trod water by his boat, too frightened to pull himself in, and a minute later the dragon went over him again, its claws full of the innkeeper's prize bull, the one that had sired the finest calves in the countryside but was so fierce it had to be staked down day and night. The bull was still twitching, and blood fell from its back thicker than rain.

The fisherman slipped his hand from the boat and went under the water, to cleanse himself of both the blood and the fear. When he surfaced again, the dragon was gone. But the fisherman stayed in the water until the cold at last drove him out, his hands as wrinkled as his grandpap's from their long soaking.

He swam to shore, forgetting both boat and line, and ran all the way back to the village leaving a wet trail. No one believed him until they saw the meadow from which the bull—chain and all—had been ripped. Then even the priest was convinced.

The healer's wife and her three daughters wept anew when they were told. And Tansy, remembering the patch of dragon's bane, blamed herself for not having guessed.

May-Ma raised her fist to the sky and screamed the old curse on dragons, remembered from years of mummery played out at planting:

Fire and water on thy wing,
The curse of God in beak and flight.

The priest tried to take the sting of her loss away. The cooper's wife was inconsolable as well, surrounded by her eleven younglings. The village men sharpened their iron pitchforks, and the old poisoned arrows that hung on the church's small apse walls were heated until the venom dripped. Tansy had to treat three boys for the flux, who had put their fingers on the arrows and then on their lips. The beekeeper got down an old book that had traveled through his family over the years called *Ye Draconis: An Historie Unnaturalis.* The only useful information therein was, "An fully-fledged draconis will suppe and digeste an bullock in fourteen days." They counted twelve days at best before the beast returned to feed again.

And then someone said, "We need a dragonslayer."

So the fisherman's son and the beekeeper's son and three other boys were sent off to see who they could find, though, as the priest thundered from the pulpit, "Beware of false heroes. Without dragons there be no need of dragonslayers."

As the boys left the village, their neighbors gathered to bid them godspeed. The sexton rang Great Tom, the treble bell that had been cast in the hundredth year after the victory over dragons. On its side was the inscription: *I am Tom, when I toll there is fire, when I thunder there is victory.* The boys carried the sound with them down the long, winding roads.

They found heroes aplenty in the towns they visited. There were men whose bravery extended to the rim of a wine cup but, sober the morning after, turned back into ploughboys, farmers, and laborers who sneaked home without a by-your-leave. They found one old general who remembered ancient wounds and would have followed them if he had had legs, but the man who carted him to and from town was too frightened to push the barrow after them. And they found a farmer's strong daughter who could lift a grown ewe under each arm but whose father forbade her to go. "One girl and five boys together on the road?" he roared. "Would that be proper? After such a trip, no one would wed her." So, though she was a head taller than her da, and forty pounds heavier, she wanted a wedding, so she stayed.

It was in a tosspot inn that the five village boys found the one they sought. They knew him for a hero the moment he stood. He moved like a god, the golden hair rippling down his back. Muscles formed like small mountains on his arms and he could make them walk from shoulder to elbow without the slightest effort. He was of a clan of gentle giants but early on had had a longing to see the world.

It did not occur to any one of the five why a hero should have sunk so low as to be cadging drinks by showing off his arms. It was enough for them that they had found him.

"Be you a hero?" breathed the fisherman's son, tracing the muscles with his eyes.

The blond man smiled, his teeth white and even. "Do I look like one?" he asked, answering question with question, making the muscles dance across his shoulders. "My name is Lancot."

The beekeeper's son looked dazzled. "That be a hero's name," he said with a sigh.

The boys shared their pennies and bought Lancot a mug of stew. He remembered things for them then:

service to a foreign queen, a battle with a walking tree, three goblins spitted on his sword. (Their blood had so pitted the blade he left it on their common grave, which was why he had it not.) On and on through the night he spun out his tales and they doled out their coin in exchange. Each thought it a fair bargain.

In the morning they caught up with him several miles down the road, his pockets a-jangle with the coins they had paid for his tales—as well as the ones they thought they had gone to bed with. They begrudged him none of it. A hero is entitled.

"Come back with us, Lancot," begged the beekeeper's son, "and we can promise you a fine living."

"More coins than ten pockets could hold," added the fisherman's son, knowing it for a small boast.

They neglected to mention the dragon, having learned that one small lesson along the way.

And the hero Lancot judged them capable of five pockets at best. Still, five was better than none, and a fine village living was better than no living at all. There was bound to be at least one pretty girl there. He was weary of the road, for the world had turned out to be no better than his home—and no worse. So he shook his head, knowing that would make his golden hair ripple all down his back. And he tensed his muscles once more for good measure. They deserved *something* for their coin.

"He is almost like . . . a god," whispered one of the boys.

Lancot smiled to himself and threw his shoulders back. He looked straight ahead. He knew he was no god. He was not even, the gods help him, a hero. Despite his posture and his muscles, he was a fraud. Heroes and gods were never afraid, and he was deadly afraid every day of his life. It was so absurd that he found himself laughing most of the time, for, by holding himself upright and smiling his hero smile, by making others party to his monstrous fraud, could he keep most of the fears at bay.

And so they arrived home, the fisherman's son, the beekeeper's son, and the three other boys alternately trailing the golden-haired hero and leading him.

They were greeted by a sobbing crowd.

The dragon, it seems, had carried off the church bell ten days before. The sexton, who had been in the act of ringing matins, had clung to the rope and had been carried away as well. Great Tom had dropped upside-down with a final dolorous knell into the bay, where it could still be seen. Little fish swam round its clapper. The sexton had not been found.

With all the sobbing and sighing, no one noticed that the hero Lancot had turned the color of scum on an ocean wave. No one, that is, except Tansy, who noticed everything, and her sister Sage, who thought that gray white was a wonderful tone for a hero's skin. "Like ice," she whispered to herself, "like the surface of a lake in winter, though his eyes are the color of a summer sky." And Rosemary, who thought he looked big enough and strong enough to train to the farm, much as a draft horse is measured for the plow.

As there was no inn and May-Ma had first claim on heroes, her husband having been the great worm's earliest meal, Lancot was put up at the healer's cottage. He eyed the three daughters with delight.

Their first dinner was a dismal affair. The healer's wife spoke of raw vengeance, Rosemary of working, Sage of romance, and Tansy of herbs. Lancot spoke not at all. In this place of dragons he knew he dared not tell his tales.

But finally Tansy took pity on his silence and asked him what, besides being a hero, he liked to do.

It being a direct question, Lancot had to answer. He thought a bit. Playing a hero had taken up all his adult time. At last he spoke. "When I was a boy . . ."

Sage sighed prettily, as if being a boy were the noblest occupation in the world.

"When I was a boy," Lancot said again, "I liked to fly kites."

"A useless waste of sticks and string," said Rosemary.

Sage sighed.

But as May-Ma cleared the table, Tansy nodded. "A link with earth and sky," she said. "As if you, too, were flying."

"If we were meant to fly," reminded Rosemary, "we would have been born with a beak . . ."

Sage laughed, a tinkling sound.

"And a longing for worms. Yes, I know," interrupted Tansy. "But little worms are useful creatures for turning the soil. It is only the great worms who are our enemies."

Rosemary's mouth thinned down.

Lancot said uneasily, "Kites . . ." then stopped. Dinner was over and the need for conversation was at an end.

In the morning the boys, backed up by their fathers, came to call. Morning being a hero's time, they came quite early. Lancot was still asleep.

"I will wake him," volunteered Sage. Her voice was so eager the fisherman's son bit his lip, for he had long loved her from afar.

Sage went into the back room and touched the sleeping hero on the shoulder. Lancot turned on the straw mattress but did not open his eyes.

"Never mind," said Rosemary urgently when Sage returned without him. "I shall do it."

She strode into the room and clapped her hands loudly right behind his left ear. Lancot sat up at once.

"Your followers are here," she snapped. "Tramping in mud and knocking the furniture about." She began to fluff up the pillow before the print of Lancot's head even had time to fade.

Reluctantly he rose, splashed drops of cold water on his cheeks, and went to face the boys.

"Do we go today?" asked the fisherman's son, quick to show his eagerness to Sage.

"Is it swords or spears?" asked the innkeeper's son.

"Or the poisoned arrows?"

"Or rocks?"

"Or . . ."

"Let me think," said Lancot, waving them into silence. "A dragon needs a plan."

"A plan," said all the boys and their fathers at once.

"Come back tomorrow and I will have a plan," said Lancot. "Or better yet, the day *after* tomorrow."

The boys nodded, but the beekeeper spoke timidly. "The day after tomorrow will be too late. The great worm is due to return to feed. The sexton was . . ." he swallowed noisily, ". . . a puny man." Unconsciously his hand strayed to his own ample waist.

Lancot closed his eyes and nodded as if he were considering a plan, but what he was really thinking about was escape. When he opened his eyes again, the boys and their fathers were gone. But Rosemary was holding the broom in a significant manner, and so Lancot put his head down as if in thought and strode from the house without even worrying about breaking his fast.

He turned down the first wooded path he came to, which was the path that wound down towards the river. He scarcely had time for surprise when the wood opened into the broad, meandering waterway, dotted with little isles, that at the edge of sight opened into the sea. Between him and the river was a gentle marsh of reeds and rice. Clustered white florets sat like tiny clouds upon green stems. There was no boat.

"There you are," said Tansy, coming out of the woods behind him. "I have found some perfect sticks for a kite and borrowed paper from the priest. The paper has a recipe for mulberry wine on it, but he says he has much improved the ingredients and so could let me have it. And I have torn up Da's old smock for ribbons and plaited vines for a rope."

"A kite?" Lancot said wonderingly. He stared at the girl, at her river-blue eyes set in a face that seemed the color of planed wood. Yesterday she had seemed no great beauty, yet here in the wood, where she reflected the colors of earth, water, sky, she was beautiful, indeed. "A kite?" he asked again, his thoughts on her.

"Heroes move in mysterious ways," Tansy said, smiling. "And since you mentioned kites, I thought perhaps kites were teasing into your mind as part of your plan."

"My plan," Lancot repeated vaguely, letting his eyes grow misty as if in great thought. He was having trouble keeping his mind on heroics.

Suddenly he felt a touch on his hand, focused his eyes, and saw that Tansy had placed her green-stained fingers on his. *Her hands are like a wood sprite's,* he thought suddenly.

"Being a hero," Tansy said, "does not mean you need to be without fear. Only fools lack fear, and I believe you to be no fool."

He dared to look at her and whispered, "No hero either."

And having admitted it, he sank down on his heels as if suddenly free of shackles that had long held him upright.

Tansy squatted next to him. "I am no hero either," she said. "To run away is by far the most sensible thing that either of us could do. But that will not stop this great worm from devouring my village and, ultimately, our world. The very least the two of us poor, frightened un-heroes can do is to construct a plan."

They sat for a long moment in silence, looking at one another. The woods stilled around them. Then Lancot smiled and, as if on a signal, the birds burst into full throat again. Little lizards resumed their scurrying. And over the water, sailing in lazy circles, a family of cormorants began their descent.

"A kite," said Lancot. His eyes closed with sudden memory. "I met a mage once, with strange high cheekbones and straw-colored hair. He spoke in a language that jangled the ear, and he told me that in his tongue the word for kite is *drache,* dragon."

Tansy nodded slowly. "Correspondences," she said. "It is the first rule of herbalry. Like calls to like. Like draws out like." She clapped her hands together. "I *knew* there was a reason that you spoke of kites."

"Do you mean that a kite could kill a dragon? *The* dragon?" Lancot asked. "Such a small, flimsy toy?"

Tansy laced her fingers together and put her chin down on top of her hands. "Not all by itself," she said. "But perhaps there is some way that we could manipulate the kite . . ."

"I could do that!" said Lancot.

"And use it to deliver a killing blow," Tansy finished.

"But there is no way a kite could carry a spear or bend a bow or wield a sword." Lancot paused. "You do not mean to fly *me* up on the kite to do that battle." He forgot to toss his hair or dance his muscles across his shoulders, so great was his fear.

Tansy laughed and put her hands on his knee. "Lancot, I have not forgotten that you are no hero. And I am no kite handler."

He furrowed his brow. "*You* will not go up the kite string. I forbid it."

"I am not yours to forbid," Tansy said quietly. "But I am no hero either. What I had in mind was something else."

He stood then and paced while Tansy told him of her plan. The river rilled over rocks to the sea, and terns scripted warnings in the sky. Lancot listened only to the sound of Tansy's voice, and watched her fingers spell out her thoughts. When she finished, he knelt by her side.

"I will make us a great kite," he said. "A *drache.* I will need paint besides, red as blood and black as hope."

"I thought hope a lighter color," exclaimed Tansy.

"Not when one is dealing with dragons," he said.

The cooper supplied the paint. Two precious books of church receipts were torn apart for the paper because

Lancot insisted that the kite be dragon-size. The extra nappies belonging to the missing babe, the petticoats of six maidens, and the fisherman's son's favorite shirt were torn up for binding. And then the building began.

Lancot sent the boys into the woods for spruce saplings after refusing to make his muscles dance. They left sullenly with his caveat in their ears: "As the dragon is mighty, yet can sail without falling through the air, so must the wood of our kite likewise be strong yet light."

Tansy, overhearing this, nodded and muttered, "Correspondences," under her breath.

And then the hero, on his knees, under the canopy of trees, showed them how to bend the wood, soaking it in water to make it flex, binding it with the rags. He ignored the girls who stood behind him to watch his shoulders ripple as he worked.

The fisherman's son soon got the hang of it, as did the cooper's eldest daughter. Rosemary was best, grumbling at the waste of good cloth, but also proud that her fingers could so nimbly wrap the wood.

They made rounded links, the first twice as large as a man, then descending in size to the middle whose circumference was that of Great Tom's bow. From there the links became smaller till the last was a match for the priest's dinner plate.

"We could play at rings," suggested Sage brightly. Only the fisherman's son laughed.

All the while Tansy sat, cross-legged, plaiting a rope.

She used the trailing vines that snaked down from the trees and added horse hair that she culled from the local herd. She borrowed hemp and line from the fisherman's wife, but she did the braiding herself, all the while whispering a charm against the unknitting of bones.

It took a full day, but at last the links were made and stacked and Lancot called the villagers to him. "Well done," he said, patting the smallest boy on the head. Then he sent the lot of them home.

Only Tansy remained behind. "That was indeed well done," she said.

"It was *easy* done," he said. "There is nothing to fear in the making of a kite. But once *it* is finished, I will be gone."

"A hero does what a hero can," answered Tansy. "We ask no more than that." But she did not stop smiling, and Lancot took up her smile as his own.

They walked along the path together towards the house but, strange to say, they were both quite careful not to let their hands meet or to let the least little bit of their clothing touch. They only listened to the nightjar calling and the erratic beating of their own timid hearts.

The next morning, before the sun had picked out a path through the interlacing of trees, the villagers had assembled the links into the likeness of a great worm. Lancot painted a dragon's face on the largest round and colored in the rest like the long, sinewy body and tail.

The boys placed the poisoned arrowheads along the top arch of the links like the ridge of a dragon's neck. The girls tied sharpened sticks beneath, like a hundred unsheathed claws.

Then the priest blessed the stick-and-paper beast, saying:

Fly with the hopes of men to guide you,
Fly with the heart of a hero to goad you,
Fly with the spirit of God to guard you,
Blessings on you, beak and tail.

Tansy made a hole in the *drache*'s mouth, which she hemmed with a white ribbon from her own hope chest. Through that hole she strung a single long red rope. To one end of the rope she knotted a reed basket, to the other she looped a handle.

"What is the basket for?" asked May-Ma. "Why do we do this? Where will it get us? And will it bring dear Da back home?"

Rosemary and Sage comforted her, but only Tansy answered her. "It is the hero's plan," she said.

And with that, May-Ma and all the villagers, whose own questions had rested in hers, had to be content.

Then with all the children holding the links, they marched down to the farthest shore. There, on the strand, where the breezes shifted back and forth between one island and the next, they stretched out the great kite, link after link, along the sand.

Lancot tested the strings, straightening and untwisting the line. Then he wound up the guy string on Rosemary's shuttle. Looking up into the sky, one hand over his eyes, he saw that for miles there were no clouds. Even the birds were down. It was an elegant slate on which to script their challenge to the great worm.

"Links up!" he cried. And at that signal, the boys each grabbed a large link, the girls the smaller ones, and held them over their heads.

"Run from me," Lancot cried.

And the children began to run, pulling the great guy rope taut between them as they went.

Meanwhile Lancot and the village men held fast to the unwinding end, tugging it up and over their own heads.

Then the wind caught the links, lifting them into the air, till the last, smallest part of the tail was up. And the beekeeper's littlest daughter, who was holding it, was so excited she forgot to let go and was carried up and away.

"I will catch you," cried the fisherman's son to her, and she let go after a bit and fell into his arms. Sage watched admiringly and touched him on the arm, and he was so red with hope he let the child tumble out of his hands.

The wind fretted and goaded the kite, and the links began to swim through the air, faster and higher, in a sinuous dance; up over their outstretched hands, over the tops of trees, until only the long red rope curling from the mouth lay circling both ends on the ground.

"Make it fast," commanded Lancot, and the men looped the great guy around the trunk of an old, thick willow, once, twice, and then a third time for luck. Then the fisherman knotted the end and the priest threw holy water on it.

"And now?" asked Rosemary.

"And now?" asked the priest.

"And now?" echoed the rest of the villagers.

"And now you must all run off home and hide," said Lancot, for it was what Tansy had rehearsed with him. "The dragon will be here within the day."

"But what is the basket for?" asked May-Ma. "And why do we do this? And where will it get us? And will it bring your dear da back?" This last she asked to Tansy, who was guiding her down the path.

But there were no answers and so no comfort in it. All the villagers went home. Tansy alone returned to find Lancot pacing by the shore.

"I thought you would be gone," she said.

"I will be." His voice was gruff, but it broke between each word.

"Then the next work is mine," said Tansy.

"I will help." His eyes said there would be no argument.

He followed her along the shoreline till they came to the place where the river flowed out, the blue white of the swift-running water meeting the lapis of the sea.

Tansy turned upstream, wading along the water's edge. That left Lancot either the deeper water or the sand. He chose the water.

Tansy questioned him with a look.

He shrugged. "I would not have you fall in," he said.

"I can swim," she answered.

"I cannot."

She laughed and skipped onto the sand. Relieved, Lancot followed.

Suddenly Tansy stopped. She let slip the pocket of woven reeds she had tied at her waist. "Here," she said, pointing.

Between the sturdy brown cattails and the spikes of wild rice was a strangely sown pattern of grassy weeds, bloody red in color, the tops embroidered with florets of pearl and pink.

"*That* is dragon's bane?" Lancot asked. "That pretty bouquet? *That* is for our greatest need?" He snorted and bent and brushed a finger carelessly across one petal. The flower seared a bloody line across his skin. "Ow!" he cried and stuck the finger in his mouth.

"Best put some aloe on that," Tansy said, digging around in her apron pocket.

Lancot shook his head. Taking his finger from his mouth he said quickly, "No bother. It is just a little sting." Then he popped the finger back in.

Tansy laughed. "I have brought *my* mitts this time. Fireweed burns only flesh. I, too, have felt that sting." She held up her hand and he could see a string of little rounded, faded scars across her palm. "Dragons are made of flesh—under the links of mail."

Lancot reached out with his burned finger and touched each scar gently, but he did not say a word.

Taking her mitts from a deep apron pocket, Tansy drew them on. Then she grasped the fireweed stems with one hand, the flowers with the other, and snapped the blossoms from the green stalk. Little wisps of smoke rose from her mitts, but did not ignite. She put each cluster into her bag.

Lancot merely watched, alert, as if ready to help.

At last the bag was pouched full of flowers.

"It is enough," Tansy said, stripping the mitts from her hands.

Back at the beach, Tansy lowered the flying basket carefully and stuffed it full of the bane. As she hauled on the rope, sending the basket back aloft, a steady stream of smoke poured through the wicker, a hazy signal written on the cloudless sky.

"Now we wait," said Tansy.

"Now we wait *under cover*," said Lancot. He led her to a nearby narrow gulch and pulled branches of willow across from bank to bank. Then he slipped under the branches, pulling Tansy after.

"Will we have to wait long?" Tansy mused, more to herself than to Lancot.

Before he could answer, they heard a strange loud chuffing, a foreign wind through the trees, and smelled a carrion stink. And though neither of them had ever heard that sound before or smelled that smell, there was no mistaking it.

"Dragon," breathed Lancot.

"*Vermifax major*," said Tansy.

And then the sky above them darkened as the great mailed body, its stomach links scratched and blood-stained from lying on old bones, put out their sun.

Instinctively, they both cringed beneath the lacy willow leaves until the red rudder of tail sailed over. Tansy even forgot to breathe, so that when the worm was gone from sight and only the smell lingered, she drew a deep breath and nearly choked on the stench. Lancot clapped his hand so hard over her mouth he left four marks on the left side of her face and a red thumbprint high on the right cheekbone. Her only protest was to place her hand gently on his wrist.

"Oh, Tansy, forgive me, I am sorry I hurt you." Lancot bit his lip. "My strength is greater than I supposed."

"I am not sorry," she answered back. "This"—she brushed her fingers across her face—"this is but a momentary pain. If that great beast had heard me and had hurt you, the pain would go on and on and on forever."

At that moment they heard a tremendous angry scream of defiance and a strange rattling sound.

"The dragon must have seen our kite," whispered Tansy. "And like all great single beasts, he kills what he cannot court."

Lancot shifted a willow branch aside with great care, and they both blinked in the sudden light of sky.

High above them the red dragon was challenging the *drache,* voice and tail making statements that no self-respecting stranger would leave unanswered. But the kite remained mute.

The dragon screamed again and dove at the kite's smallest links, severing the last two. As the links slipped through the air, twisting and spiraling in the drafts made by the dragon's wings, the beast turned on the paper-and-stick pieces and swallowed them in a single gulp. Then, with a great surprised belch, the worm vomited up the pieces again. Crumpled, broken, mangled beyond repair, they fell straight down into the sea.

The dragon roared again, this time snapping at the head of the kite. The roar was a mighty wind that whipped the kite upward, and so the dragon's jaws closed only on the rope that held the basket of fireweed, shredding the strand. The basket and half the rope fell lazily through the air and, with a tiny splash, sank beneath the waves. At once, a high frantic hissing bubbled up through the water, and the sea boiled with the bane.

"It's gone," Tansy whispered. "The bane. It's gone." Without giving a thought for her own safety, she clambered out of the gulch and, bent over, scuttled to the trees, intent on fetching more of the precious weed. The dragon, concentrating on its skyborne foe, never saw her go.

But Lancot did, his hand reaching out too late to clutch the edge of her skirt as it disappeared over the embankment. "Tansy, no!"

She made no sign she had heard, but entered the trees and followed the stream quickly to the muddle of water and reeds that held the rest of the bane. Wading in, she began to snatch great handfuls of the stuff, heedless of the burns, until she had gathered all there was to find. Then she struggled ashore and raced back. Her wet skirts tangled in her legs as she ran.

Lancot, caught in a panic of indecision, had finally emerged from their hiding place and stared alternately at the sky and the path along the sea. When Tansy came running back, hands seared and smoking but holding the fireweed, he ran to her.

"I have gathered all there is," she said, only at the last letting her voice crack with the pain.

Lancot reached for the weed.

"No," Tansy whispered hoarsely, "take the mitts from my pocket" She added miserably, "I was in such a hurry, I forgot to put them on. And then I was in too much pain to do other."

Lancot grabbed the mitts from her pocket and forced them onto his large hands. Then he took the weed from her. She hid her burned hands behind her back.

"How will I get these up to the dragon?" asked Lancot suddenly, for the question had not occurred to either of them before.

They turned as one and stared at the sky.

It was the dragon itself that gave them the answer then, for, as they watched, it grabbed a great mouthful of the kite and raged at it, pulling hard against the line that tethered the *drache* to the tree. The willow shook violently with each pull.

Lancot smiled down at Tansy. "You are no hero," he said. "Your hands are too burned for that. And I am no hero, either. But . . . But . . ." His voice trembled only slightly. "As a boy I fetched many kites out of trees." And before Tansy could stop him, he kissed her forehead, careful of the bane he carried, and whispered into her hair, "And put some *hallow* on those palms."

"Aloe," she said, but he did not hear her.

Lancot transferred the bane to one mitt, slipped the mitt off his other hand, and began to shinny one-handed up the guy rope that was anchored to the underside of the kite. If the dragon, still wrestling with the *drache,* felt the extra weight, it made not the slightest sign.

Twice the dragon pulled so furiously that Lancot slipped off. And then, when he was halfway up the rope, there was a huge sucking sound. Slowly the willow was pulled up, roots and all, out of the earth. And the dragon, along with the kite, the string, Lancot, and the tree, flew east toward the farthest isles.

Tansy, screaming and screaming, watched them go.

As they whipped through the air, Lancot continued his slow crawl up the rope. Once or twice the fireweed brushed his cheek and he gritted his teeth against the pain. And once a tiny floret touched his hair, and the single strand sizzled down to his scalp. The smell of that was awful. But he did not drop the weeds, nor did he relinquish his hold on the guy rope. Up and up he inched as the dragon, its limp paper prey in its claws, pulled them toward its home.

They were closing in on the farthest island, a sandy lozenge shape resting in the blue sea, when Lancot's bare hand touched the bottom of the kite and the cold golden nail of the dragon's claw. He could feel his heart hammering hard against his chest, and the skin rippled faster along his shoulders and neck than ever he could have made the muscles dance. He could feel the wind whistling past his bared teeth, could feel the tears teasing from his eyes. He remembered Tansy's voice saying "I can swim," and his own honest reply. Smiling ruefully, he thought, "I shall worry about that anon." Then he slipped his arm around the dragon's leg, curved his legs up and around, until he could kneel. He dared not look down again.

He stood and at last the dragon seemed to take notice of him. It clenched and unclenched its claw. The kite and tree fell away, tumbling, it seemed, forever till they plunged into the sea, sending up a splash that could be seen from all the islands.

Lancot looked up just in time to see the great head of the beast bend curiously around to examine its own feet. It was an awkward move in the air, and for a moment worm and man plummeted downward.

Then the dragon opened its great furnace jaws, the spikes of teeth as large as tree trunks, as sharp as swords.

Lancot remembered his boyhood and the games of sticks and balls. He snatched up the fireweed with his ungloved hand and, ignoring the sting of it, flung the lot into the dragon's maw.

Surprised, the dragon swallowed, then straightened up and began to roar.

Lancot was no fool. He put the mitt over his eyes, held his nose with his burned hand, and jumped.

On shore, Tansy had long since stopped screaming to watch the precarious climb. Each time Lancot slipped she felt her heart stutter. She prayed he might drop off before the dragon noticed, until she remembered he could not swim.

When he reached the dragon's foot, Tansy was wading into the water, screaming once again. Her aloe-smeared hands had left marks on her skirts, on her face.

And when the tree and kite fell, she felt her hopes rise until she saw that Lancot was not with them. She prayed then, the only prayer she could conjure up, the one her mother had spoken:

Fire and water on thy wing,
The curse of God in beak and flight.

It seemed to her much too small a prayer to challenge so great and horrible a beast.

And then the dragon turned on itself, curling around to look at Lancot, and they began to tumble toward the sea.

At that point Tansy no longer knew what prayers might work. "Fly!" she screamed. "Drop!" she screamed.

No sooner had she called out the last than the dragon straightened out and roared so loudly she had to put her hands over her ears, heedless of the aloe smears in her hair. Then, as she watched, the great dragon began to burn. Its body seemed touched by a red aureole and flames flickered the length of it, from mouth to tail. Quite suddenly, it seemed to go out, guttering like a candle, from the back forward. Black scabs fell from its tail, its legs, its back, its head. It turned slowly around in the air, as if each movement brought pain, and then Tansy could see its head. Only its eyes held life till the very end when, with a blink, the life was gone. The dragon drifted, floated down onto a sandbar, and lay like a mountain of ash. It was not a fierce ending but rather a gigantic sigh, and Tansy could not believe how unbearably sad it made her feel, as if she and the dragon and Lancot, too, had been cheated of some reward for their courage. She thought, quite suddenly, of a child's balloon at a fair pricked by a needle, and she wept.

A hand on her shoulder recalled her to the place. It was the fisherman's son.

"Gone then?" he asked. He meant the dragon.

But knowing Lancot was gone as well, Tansy began sobbing anew. Neither her mother nor her sisters nor the priest nor all the celebrations that night in the town could salve her. She walked down to the water's edge at dusk by herself and looked out over the sea to the spit of land where the ash mound that had been the dragon was black against the darkening sky.

The gulls were still. From behind her a solitary owl called its place from tree to tree. A small breeze teased into the willows, setting them to rustling. Tansy heard a noise near her and shrugged further into herself. She would let no one pull her out of her misery, not her mother nor her sisters nor all the children of the town.

"I could use a bit of *hallow* on my throwing hand," came a voice.

"Aloe," she said automatically before she turned.

"It's awfully hard to kill a hero," said Lancot with a smile.

"But you can't swim."

"It's low tide," he said. "And I *can* wade."

Tansy laughed.

"It's awfully hard to kill a hero," so said Lancot. "But we ordinary fellows, we do get hurt. So I could use a bit of *hallow* on my hand."

She didn't mind the smear of aloe on her hair and cheek. But that came later on, much later that night. And it seemed to the two of them that what they did then was very heroic indeed.

There is a spit of land near the farthest shores of the farthest islands. It is known as Dragonfield. Once dragons dwelt on the isles in great herds, feeding on the dry brush and fueling their flames with the carcasses of small animals and migratory birds. There are no dragons there now, though the nearer islands are scored with long furrows as though giant claws had been at work, and the land is fertile from the bones of the buried behemoths. There is a large mount of ash-colored rock that appears and disappears in the ebb and flow of the tide. No birds land on that rock, and seals avoid it as well. The islanders call it Worm's Head, and once a year they row out to it and sail a great kite from its highest point, a kite that they then set afire and let go into the prevailing winds. Some of the younger mothers complain that one day that kite will burn down a house, and they have agitated to end the ceremony. But as long as the story of Tansy and the hero is told, the great kites will fly over the rock, of that I am sure.

THE SWORD AND THE STONE

"Would you believe a sword in a stone, my liege?" the old necromancer asked. "I dreamed of one last night. Stone white as whey with a sword stuck in the top like a knife through butter. It means something. My dreams always mean something. Do you believe that stone and that sword, my lord?"

The man on the carved wooden throne sighed heavily, his breath causing the hairs of his moustache to flap. "Merlinnus, I have no time to believe in a sword in a stone. Or on a stone. Or under a stone. I'm just too damnably tired for believing today. And you *always* have dreams."

"This dream is different, my liege."

"They're always different. But I've just spent half a morning pacifying two quarreling *dux bellorum.* Or is it *bellori?*"

"Belli," muttered the mage, shaking his head.

"Whatever. And sorting out five counterclaims from my chief cook and his mistresses. He should stick to his kitchen. His affairs are a mess. And awarding grain to a lady whose miller maliciously killed her cat. Did you know, Merlinnus, that we actually have a law about cat killing that levies a fine of the amount of grain that will cover the dead cat completely when it is held up by the tip of its tail and its nose touches the ground? It took over a peck of grain." He sighed again.

"A large cat, my lord," mumbled the mage.

"A *very* large cat indeed," agreed the King, letting his head sink into his hands. "And a *very* large lady. With a lot of *very* large and important lands. Now what in Mithras's name do I want a sword and a stone for when I have to deal with all that?"

"In *Christ's* name, my lord. *Christ's* name. Remember, we are Christians now." The mage held up a gnarled forefinger. "And it is a sword *in* a stone."

"*You* are the Christian," the King said. "*I* still drink bull's blood with my men. It makes them happy, though the taste of it is somewhat less than good wine." He laughed mirthlessly. "And yet I wonder how good a Christian you are, Merlinnus, when you still insist on talking to trees. Oh, there are those who have seen you walking in your wood and talking, always talking, even though there is no one there. Once a Druid, always a Druid, so Sir Kai says."

"Kai is a fool," answered the old man, crossing himself

quickly, as if marking the points of the body punctuated his thought.

"Kai is a fool, indeed, but even fools have ears and eyes. Go away, Merlinnus, and do not trouble me with this sword on a stone. I have more important things to deal with." He made several dismissing movements with his left hand while summoning the next petitioner with his right. The petitioner, a young woman with a saucy smile and a bodice bouncing with promises, moved forward. The King smiled back.

Merlinnus left and went outside, walking with more care than absolutely necessary, to the grove beyond the castle walls where his favorite oak grew. He addressed it rather informally, they being of a long acquaintance.

"*Salve, amice frondifer,* greetings, friend leaf bearer. What am I to do with that boy? When I picked him out, it was because the blood of a strong-minded and lusty king ran in his veins, though on the sinister side. Should I then have expected gratitude and imagination to accompany such a heritage? Ah, but unfortunately I did. My brains must be rotting away with age. Tell me, *de glande nate,* sprout of an acorn, do I ask too much? Vision! That's what is missing, is it not?"

A rustle of leaves, as if a tiny wind puzzled through the grove, was his only answer.

Merlinnus sat down at the foot of the tree and rubbed his back against the bark, easing an itch that had been there since breakfast. He tucked the skirt of his woolen robe between his legs and stared at his feet. He still favored the Roman summer sandals, even into late fall, because closed boots tended to make the skin between his toes crackle like old parchment. And besides, in the heavy boots, his feet sweated and stank. But he always felt cold now, winter and summer. So he wore a woolen robe year-round.

"Did I address him incorrectly, do you think? These new kings are such sticklers for etiquette. An old man like me finds that stuff boring. Such a waste of time, and time is the one commodity I have little of." He rubbed a finger alongside his nose.

"I thought to pique his interest, to get him wondering about a sword that is stuck in a stone like a knife in a slab of fresh beef. A bit of legerdemain, that, and I'm rather proud of it actually. You see, it wasn't *just* a dream. I've done it up in my tower room. Anyone with a bit of knowledge can read the old Latin building manuals and construct a ring of stones. Building the baths under the castle was harder work. But that sword in the stone—yes, I'm rather proud of it. And what that young king must realize is that he needs to do something more than rule on cases of quarreling dukes and petty mistresses and grasping rich widows. He has to . . ." Stopping for a minute to listen to the wind again through trees, Merlinnus shook his head and went on. "He has to fire up these silly tribes, give them something magical to rally them. I don't mean him to be just another petty chieftain. Oh, no. He's to be my greatest creation, that boy." He rubbed his nose again. "My last creation, I'm afraid.

If this one doesn't work out, what am I to do?"

The wind, now stronger, soughed through the trees.

"I was given just thirty-three years to bind this kingdom, you know. That's the charge, the geas laid on me: thirty-three years to bind it *per crucem et quercum,* by cross and by oak. And this, alas, is the last year."

A cuckoo called down from the limb over his head.

"The first one I tried was that idiot Uther. Why, his head was more wood than thine." The old man chuckled to himself. "And then there were those twins from the Hebrides who enjoyed games so much. Then that witch, Morgana. She made a pretty mess of things. I even considered—at her prompting—her strange, dark little son. Or was he her nephew? I forget which. When one has been a lifelong celibate as I, one tends to dismiss such frequent and casual couplings and their messy aftermaths as unimportant. But that boy had a sly, foxy look about him. Nothing would follow him but a pack of dogs. And then I found this one right under my nose. In some ways he's the dullest of the lot, and yet in a king dullness can be a virtue. *If* the crown is secure."

A nut fell on his head, tumbled down his chest, and landed in his lap. It was a walnut, which was indeed strange, since he was sitting beneath an oak. Expecting magic, the mage looked up. There was a little red squirrel staring down at him. Merlinnus cracked the nut between two stones, extracted the meat, and held up half to the squirrel.

"Walnuts from acorn trees," he said. As soon as the squirrel had snatched away its half of the nutmeat, the old man drifted off into a dream-filled sleep.

"Wake up, wake up, old one." It was the shaking, not the sentence, that woke him. He opened his eyes. A film of sleep lent a soft focus to his vision. The person standing over him seemed haloed in mist.

"Are you all right, Grandfather?" The voice was soft, too.

Merlinnus sat up. He was, he guessed, too old to be sleeping out of doors. The ground cold had seeped into his bones. Like an old tree, his sap ran sluggishly. But being caught out by a youngster made him grumpy. "Why shouldn't I be all right?" he answered, more gruffly than he meant.

"You are so thin, Grandfather, and you sleep so silently. I feared you dead. One should not die in a sacred grove. It offends the Goddess."

"Are you then a worshiper of the White One?" he asked, carefully watching the stranger's hands. No true worshiper would answer that question in a straightforward manner, but would instead signal the dark secret with an inconspicuous semaphore. But all that the fingers signed were concern for him. Forefinger, fool's finger, physic's finger, and ear finger were silent of secrets. Merlinnus sighed and struggled to sit upright.

The stranger put a hand under his arm and back and gently eased him into a comfortable position. Once up, Merlinnus took a better look. The stranger was a boy with that soft lambent cheek not yet coarsened by a beard. His eyes were the clear blue of speedwells. The eyebrows were dark swallow wings, sweeping high and back toward luxuriant and surprisingly gold hair caught under a dark cap. He was dressed in homespun but neat and clean. His hands, clasped before him, were small and well formed.

Sensing the mage's inspection, the boy spoke. "I have come in the hopes of becoming a page at court." Then he added, "I wish to learn the sword and lance."

Merlinnus's mouth screwed about a bit but at last settled into a passable smile. Perhaps he could find some use for the boy. A wedge properly placed had been known to split a mighty tree. And he had so little time. "What is your name, boy?"

"I am called . . ." There was a hesitation, scarcely noticeable. "Gawen."

Merlin's smile broadened. "Ah, but we have already a great knight by a similar name. He is praised as one of the King's Three Fearless Men."

"Fearless in bed, certainly," the boy answered. "The hollow man." Then, as if to soften his words, he added, "Or so it is said where I come from."

So, Merlinnus thought, *there may be more to this than a child come to court.* Aloud, he said, "And where *do* you come from?"

The boy looked down and smoothed the homespun where it lay against his thighs. "The coast."

Refusing to comment that the coast was many miles long, both north and south, Merlinnus said sharply, "Do not condemn a man with another's words. And do not praise him that way, either."

The boy did not answer.

"Purity in tongue must precede purity in body," the mage added, for the boy's silence annoyed him. "That is my first lesson to you."

A small sulky voice answered him. "I am too old for lessons."

"None of us is too old," said Merlinnus, wondering why he felt so compelled to go on and on. Then, as if to soften his criticism, he added, "Even I learned something today."

"And that is . . ."

"It has to do with the Matter of Britain," the mage said, "and is therefore beyond you."

"Why beyond me?"

"Give me your hand." He held his own out, crabbed with age.

Gawen reluctantly put his small hand forward, and the mage ran a finger across the palm, slicing the lifeline where it forked early.

"I see you are no stranger to work. The calluses tell me that. But what work it is I do not know."

Gawen withdrew his hand and smiled brightly, his mouth wide, mobile, telling of obvious relief.

Merlinnus wondered what other secrets the hand might have told him, could he have read palms as easily as a village herb wife. Then, shaking his head, he stood.

"Come. Before I bring you into court, let us go and wash ourselves in the river."

The boy's eyes brightened. "*You* can bring me to court?"

With more pride than he felt and more hope than he had any right to feel, Merlinnus smiled. "Of course, my son. After all, I am the High King's mage."

They walked companionably to the river, which ran noisily between stones. Willows on the bank wept their leaves into the swift current. Merlinnus used the willow trunks for support as he sat down carefully on the bank. He eased his feet, sandals and all, into the cold water. It was too fast and too slippery for him to stand.

"Bring me enough to bathe with," he said, pointing to the water. It could be a test of the boy's quick-wittedness.

Gawan stripped off his cap, knelt down, and held the cap in the river. Then he pulled it out and wrung the water over the old man's hands.

Merlinnus liked that. The job had been done, and quickly, with little wasted motion. Another boy might have plunged into the river, splashing like an untrained animal. Or asked what to do.

The boy muttered, "*De matro ad patri.*"

Startled, Merlinnus looked up into the clear, untroubled blue eyes. "You know Latin?"

"Did I . . . did I say it wrong?"

"'From the mother to the father.'"

"That is what I meant." Gawen's young face was immediately transformed by the wide smile. "The . . . the brothers taught me."

Merlinnus knew of only two monasteries along the coast and they were both very far away. The sisters of Quintern Abbey were much closer, but they never taught boys. *This child,* thought the mage, *has come a very long way indeed.* Aloud, he said, "They taught you well."

Gawen bent down again, dipped the cap once more, and this time used the water to wash his own face and hands. Then he wrung the cap out thoroughly but did not put it back on his head. Cap in hand, he faced the mage. "You *will* bring me to the High King, then?"

A sudden song welled up in Merlinnus's breast, a high hallelujah so unlike any of the dark chantings he was used to under the oaks. "I will," he said.

As they neared the castle, the sun was setting. It was unusually brilliant, rain and fog being the ordinary settings for evenings in early fall. The high tor, rumored to be hollow, was haloed with gold and loomed up behind the topmost towers.

Gawen gasped at the high timbered walls.

Merlinnus smiled to himself but said nothing. For a child from the coast, such walls must seem near miraculous. But for the competent architect who planned for eternity, mathematics was miracle enough. He had long studied the writing of the Roman builders, whose prose styles were as tedious as their knowledge was great. He had learned from them how to instruct men in the slotting of breastwork timbers. All he had needed was the ability to read—and time. Yet time, he thought bitterly, for construction as with everything else, had all but run out for him. Still, there was this boy—and this *now.*

"Come," said the mage. "Stand tall and enter."

The boy squared his shoulders, and boy and mage hammered upon the carved wooden doors together.

Having first checked them out through the spyhole, the guards opened the doors with a desultory air that marked them at the end of their watch.

"*Ave* Merlinnus," said one guard with an execrable accent. It was obvious he knew that much Latin and no more. The other guard was silent.

Gawen was silent as well, but his small silence was filled with wonder. Merlinnus glanced slantwise and saw the boy taking in the great stoneworks, the Roman mosaic panel on the entry wall, all the fine details he had insisted upon. He remembered the argument with Morgana when they had built that wall.

"An awed emissary," he had told her, "is already half won over."

At least she had had the wit to agree, though later

those same wits had been addled by drugs and wine and the gods only knew what other excesses. Merlinnus shook his head. It was best to look forward, not back, when you had so little time. Looking backward was an old man's drug.

He put his hand on the boy's shoulder, feeling the fine bones beneath the jerkin. "Turn here," he said softly.

They turned into the long, dark walkway where the walls were niched for the slide of three separate portcullises. No invaders could break in this way. Merlinnus was proud of the castle's defenses.

As they walked, Gawen's head was constantly aswivel: left, right, up, down. Wherever he had come from had left him unprepared for this. At last the hall opened into an inner courtyard where pigs, poultry, and wagons vied for space.

Gawen breathed out again. "It's like home," he whispered.

"Eh?" Merlinnus let out a whistle of air like a skin bag deflating.

"Only finer, of course." The quick answer was almost satisfying, but not quite. Not quite. And Merlinnus was not one to enjoy unsolved puzzles.

"To the right," the old man growled, shoving his finger hard into the boy's back. "To the right."

They were ushered into the throne room without a moment's hesitation. This much, at least, a long memory and a reputation for magic-making and king-making brought him.

The King looked up from the paper he was laboriously reading, his finger marking his place. He always, Merlinnus noted with regret, read well behind that finger, for he had come to reading as a grown man, and reluctantly, his fingers faster in all activities than his mind. But he *was* well meaning, the mage reminded himself. Just a bit sluggish on the uptake. A king should be faster than his advisors, though he seem to lean upon them; quicker than his knights, though he seem to send them on ahead.

"Ah, Merlinnus, I am glad you are back. There's a dinner tonight with an emissary from the Orkneys and you know I have trouble understanding their rough mangling of English. You will be there?"

Merlinnus nodded.

"And there is a contest I need your advice on. Here." He snapped his fingers and a list was put into his hand. "The men want to choose a May Queen to serve next year. I think they are hoping to thrust her on me as my queen. They have drawn up a list of those qualities they think she should possess. Kai wrote the list down."

Kai, Merlinnus thought disagreeably, was the only one of that crew who *could* write, and his spelling was only marginally better than his script. He took the list and scanned it:

Thre thingges smalle-headde, nose, breestes;
Thre thingges largge-waiste, hippes, calves;
Thre thingges longge-haires, finggers, thies;

Thre thingges short-height, toes, utterance.

"Sounds more like an animal in a bestiary than a girl, my lord," Merlinnus ventured at last.

Gawen giggled.

"They are trying . . ." the King began.

"They certainly are," muttered the mage.

"They are trying . . . to be helpful, Merlinnus." The King glowered at the boy by the mage's side. "And who is this fey bit of work?"

The boy bowed deeply. "I am called Gawen, Sire, and I have come to learn to be a knight."

The King ground his teeth. "And some of them, no doubt, will like you be-nights."

A flush spread across the boy's cheeks. "I am sworn to the Holy Mother to be pure," he said.

"Are you a Grailer or a Goddess worshiper?" Before the boy could answer, the King turned to Merlinnus. "Is he well bred?"

"Of course," said Merlinnus, guessing. The Latin and the elegant speech said as much, even without the slip about how much a castle looked like home.

"Very well," the King said, arching his back and putting one hand behind him. "Damned throne's too hard. I think I actually prefer a soldier's pallet. Or a horse." He stood and stretched. "That's enough for one day. I will look at the rest tomorrow." He put out a hand and steadied himself, using the mage's shoulder, then descended the two steps to the ground.

Speaking into Merlinnus's right ear because he knew the left ear was a bit deafened by age, the King said, "When you gave me the kingdom, you forgot to mention that kings need to sit all day long. You neglected to tell me about wooden thrones. If you had told me that when you offered me the crown, I might have thought about it a bit longer."

"And would you have made a different choice, my lord?" asked Merlinnus quietly.

The King laughed and said aloud, "No, but I would have requested a different throne."

Merlinnus looked shocked. "But that is the High King's throne. Without it, you would not be recognized."

The King nodded.

Gawen, silent until this moment, spoke up. "Would not a cushion atop the throne do? Like the crown atop the High King's head?"

The King's hand went immediately to the heavy circlet of metal on his head. Then he swept it off, shook out his long blond locks, and laughed. "Of course. A cushion. Out of the mouth of babes . . . It would do, would it not, Merlinnus?"

The mage's mouth twisted about the word. "Cushion." But he could think of no objection. It was the quiet homeyness of the solution that offended him. But certainly it would work.

Merlinnus put aside his niggling doubts about the boy Gawen and turned instead to the problem at hand: making the King accept the magic of the sword in the stone.

"I beg you, Sire," the old mage said the next morning, "to listen." He accompanied his request with a bow on bended knee. The pains of increasing age were only slightly mitigated by some tisanes brewed by a local herb wife. Merlinnus sighed heavily as he went down. It was that sigh, sounding so much like his old grandfather's, that decided the King.

"All right, all right, Merlinnus. Let us see this sword and this stone."

"It is in my workroom," Merlinnus said. "If you will accompany me there." He tried to stand and could not.

"I will not only accompany you," said the King patiently, "it looks as if I will have to carry you." He came down from his throne and lifted the old man up to his feet.

"I can walk," Merlinnus said somewhat testily.

Arm in arm, they wound through the castle halls, up three flights of stone stairs to Merlinnus's tower workroom.

The door opened with a spoken spell and three keys. The King seemed little impressed.

"There!" said the mage, pointing to a block of white marble with veins of red and green running through. Sticking out of the stone top was the hilt of a sword. The hilt was carved with wonderful runes. On the white marble face was the legend:

WHOSO PULLETH OUTE
THIS SWERD OF THIS STONE
IS RIGHTWYS KYNGE BORNE OF
ALL BRYT A YGNE

Slowly the King read aloud, his finger tracing the letters in the stone. When he had finished, he looked up. "But *I* am king of all Britain."

"Then pull the sword, Sire."

The King smiled and it was not a pleasant smile. He was a strong man, in his prime, and except for his best friend, Sir Lancelot, he was reputed to be the strongest in the kingdom. It was one of the reasons Merlinnus had chosen him. He put his hand to the hilt, tightened his fingers around it until the knuckles were white, and pulled.

The sword remained in the stone.

"Merlinnus, this is witchery. I will not have it." The King's voice was cold.

"And with *witchery* you will pull it out, in full view of the admiring throngs. You—and no one else." The mage smiled benignly.

The King let go of the sword. "But why this? I am *already* king."

"Because I hear grumblings in the kingdom. Oh, do not look slantwise at me, boy. It is not magic but reliable spies that tell me so. There are those who refuse to follow you, to be bound to you, and so bind this kingdom, because they doubt the legitimacy of your claim."

The King snorted. "And they are right, Merlinnus. I am king because the archmage wills it. *Per crucem et quercum.*"

Startled, Merlinnus asked, "How did you know that?"

"Oh, my old friend, do you think you are the only one with reliable spies?"

Merlinnus stared into the King's eyes. "Yes, you are right. You are king because I willed it. And because you earned it. But this bit of legerdemain . . ."

"Witchery!" interrupted the King.

Merlinnus persisted. "This *legerdemain* will have them all believing in you." He added quickly, "As I do. *All* of them. To bind the kingdom you need *all* the tribes to follow you."

The King looked down and then, as if free of the magic for a moment, turned and stared out of the tower window to the north, where winter was already creeping down the mountainsides. "Do those few tribes matter? The ones who paint themselves blue and squat naked around small fires? The ones who wrap themselves in woolen blankets and blow noisily into animal bladders, calling it song? The ones who dig out shelled fish with their toes and eat the fish raw? Do we really want to bring them to our kingdom?"

"They are all part of Britain. The Britain of which you are the king now and for the future."

The King shifted his gaze from the mountains to the guards walking his donjon walls. "Are you positive I shall be able to draw the sword? I will *not* be made a mockery to satisfy some hidden purpose of yours."

"Put your hand on the sword, Sire."

The King turned slowly, as if the words had a power to command him. He walked back to the marble. It seemed to glow. He reached out and then, before his hand touched the hilt, by an incredible act of will, he stopped. "I am a good soldier, Merlinnus. And I love this land."

"I know."

With a resonant slap the King's hand grasped the sword. Merlinnus muttered something in a voice as soft as a cradle song. The sword slid noiselessly from the stone.

Holding the sword above his head, the King turned and looked steadily at the mage. "If I were a wicked man, I would bring this down on your head. Now."

"I know."

Slowly the sword descended, and when it was level with his eyes, the King put his left hand to the hilt as well. He hefted the sword several times and made soft comfortable noises deep in his chest. Then carefully, like a woman threading a needle, he slid the sword back into its slot in the stone.

"I will have my men take this and place it before the great cathedral so that all might see it. *All* my people shall have a chance to try their hands."

"All?"

"Even the ones who paint themselves blue or blow into bladders or do other disgusting and uncivilized things." The King smiled. "I shall even let mages try."

Merlinnus smiled back. "Is that wise?"

"I am the one with the strong arm, Merlinnus. You are to provide the wisdom. And the witchery."

"Then let the mages try, too," Merlinnus said. "For all the good it will do them."

"It is a fine sword, Merlinnus. It shall honor its wielder." He put his hand back on the hilt and heaved. The sword did not move.

The soldiers, with no help from Merlinnus, moaned and pushed and sweated and pulled until at last they managed to remove the sword-and-stone with a series of rollers and ropes. At the King's request it was set up in front of the great cathedral in the center of the town, outside the castle walls. News of it was carried by carters and jongleurs, gleemen and criers, from castle to castle and town to town. Within a month the hilt of the sword was filthy from the press of hundreds of hands. It seemed that in the countryside there were many who would be king.

Young Gawen took it upon himself to clean the hilt whenever he had time. He polished the runes on the stone lovingly, too, and studied the white marble from all angles. But he never put his hand to the sword as if to pull it. When the King was told of this, he smiled and his hand strayed to the cushion beneath him.

Gawen reported on the crowds around the stone to Merlinnus as he recounted his other lessons.

"Helm, aventail, bymie, gauntlet, cuisses . . ." he recited, touching the parts of his body where the armor would rest. "And, archmage, there was a giant of a man there today, dressed all in black, who tried the sword. And six strange tribesmen with blue skin and necklaces of shells. Two of them tried to pull together. The sword would not come out, but their blue dye came off. I had a horrible time scrubbing it from the hilt. And Sir Kai came."

"Again?"

The boy laughed. "It was his sixth try. He waits until it is dinnertime and no one is in the square."

The old mage nodded at every word. "Tell me again."

"About Sir Kai?"

"About the parts of the armor. You must have the lesson perfect for tomorrow."

The boy's mouth narrowed as he began. "Helm, aventail . . ."

At each word, Merlinnus felt a surge of pride and puzzlement. Though the recitation was an old one, it sounded new and somehow different in Gawen's mouth.

They waited until the night of the solstice, when the earth sat poised between night and night. Great bonfires were lit in front of the cathedral to drive back the darkness, while inside candles were lighted to do the same.

"It is time," Merlinnus said to the King, without any preliminaries.

"It is always time," answered the King, placing his careful marks on the bottom of yet another piece of parchment.

"I mean time to pull the sword from the stone." Merlinnus offered his hand to the King.

Pushing aside the offer, the King rose.

"I see you use the cushion now," Merlinnus said.

"It helps somewhat." He stretched. "I only wish I had two of them."

The mage shook his head. "You are the King. Command the second."

The King looked at him steadily. "I doubt such excess is wise."

Remembering Morgana, the mage smiled.

They walked arm in arm to the waiting horses. Merlinnus was helped onto a grey whose broad back was more like a chair than a charger. But then, he had always been ill at ease on horseback. And horses, even the ones with the calmest dispositions, sensed some strangeness in him. They always shied.

The King strode to his own horse, a barrel-chested bay with a smallish head. It had been his mount when he was a simple soldier and he had resisted all attempts to make him ride another.

"Mount up," the King called to his guards.

Behind him his retinue mounted. Sir Kai was the first to vault into the saddle. Young Gawen, astride a pony that was a present from the King, was the last.

With a minimum of fuss, they wound along the path down the hillside toward the town, and only the clopping of hooves on dirt marked their passage. Ahead were torchbearers and behind them came the household, each with a candle. So light came to light, a wavering parade to the waiting stone below.

In the fire-broken night the white stone gleamed before the black hulk of the cathedral. The darker veins in the stone meandered like faery streams across its surface. The sword, now shadow, now light, was the focus of hundreds of eyes. And, as if pulled by some invisible string, the King rode directly to the stone, dismounted, and knelt before it. Then he removed his circlet of office and shook free the long golden mane it had held so firmly in place. When he stood again, he put the crown on the top of the stone so that it lay just below the angled sword.

The crowd fell still.

"This crown and this land belong to the man who can pull the sword from the stone," the King said, his voice booming into the strange silence. "So it is written—here." He gestured broadly with his hand toward the runes.

"Read it," cried a woman's voice from the crowd.

"We want to hear it," shouted another.

A man's voice, picking up her argument, dared a further

step. "We want the mage to read it." Anonymity lent his words power. The crowd muttered its agreement.

Merlinnus dismounted carefully and, after adjusting his robes, walked to the stone. He glanced only briefly at the words on its side, then turned to face the people.

"The message on the stone is burned here," he said, pointing to his breast, "here in my heart. It says, *Whoso pulleth out this sword of this stone is rightwise king born of all Britain.*"

Sir Kai nodded and said loudly, "Yes, that is what it says. Right."

The King put his hands on his hips. "And so, good people, the challenge has been thrown down before us all. He who would be king of all Britain must step forward and put his hand on the sword."

At first there was no sound at all but the dying echo of the King's voice. Then a child cried and that started the crowd. They began talking to one another, jostling, arguing, some good-naturedly and others with a belligerent tone. Finally, a rather sheepish farm boy, taller by almost a head than Sir Kai, who was the tallest of the knights, was thrust from the crowd. He had a shock of wheat-colored hair over one eye and a dimple in his chin.

"I'd try, my lord," he said. He was plainly uncomfortable, having to talk to the King. "I mean, it wouldn't do no harm."

"No harm indeed, son," said the King. He took the boy by the elbow and escorted him to the stone.

The boy put both his hands around the hilt and then stopped. He looked over his shoulder at the crowd. Someone shouted encouragement and then the whole push of people began to call out to him.

"Do it. Pull the bastard. Give it a heave. Haul it out." Their cries came thick now and, buoyed by their excitement, the boy put his right foot up against the stone. Then he leaned backward and pulled. His hands slipped along the hilt and he fell onto his bottom, to the delight of the crowd.

Crestfallen, the boy stood up. He stared unhappily at his worn boots, as if he did not know where else to look or how to make his feet carry him away.

The King put his hand on the boy's shoulder. "What is your name, son?" The gentleness in his voice silenced the crowd's laughter.

"Percy, sir," the boy managed at last.

"Then, Percy," said the King, "because you were brave enough to try where no one else would set hand on the sword, you shall come to the castle and learn to be one of my knights."

"Maybe not *your* knight," someone shouted from the crowd.

A shadow passed over the King's face and he turned toward the mage.

Merlinnus shook his head imperceptibly and put his finger to his lips.

The King shifted his gaze back to the crowd. He smiled. "No, perhaps not. We shall see. Who else would try?"

At last Sir Kai brushed his hand across his breastplate. He alone of the court still affected the Roman style. Tugging his gloves down so that the fingers fit snugly, he walked to the stone and placed his right hand on the hilt. He gave it a slight tug, smoothed his golden moustache with the fingers of his left hand, then reached over with his left hand and with both gave a mighty yank. The sword did not move.

Kai shrugged and turned toward the King. "But I am still first in your service," he said.

"And in my heart, brother," acknowledged the King.

Then, one by one, the knights lined up and took turns pulling on the sword. Stocky Bedevere; handsome Gawain; Tristan, maned like a lion; cocky Galahad; and the rest. But the sword, ever firm in its stone scabbard, never moved.

At last, of all the court's knights, only Lancelot was left.

"And you, good Lance, my right hand, the strongest of us all, will you not try?" asked the King.

Lancelot, who disdained armor except in battle and was dressed in a simple tunic, the kind one might dance in, shook his head. "I have no wish to be king. I only wish to be of service."

The King walked over to him and put his hand on Lancelot's shoulder. He whispered into the knight's ear. "It is the stone's desire, not ours, that will decide this. But if you do *not* try, then my leadership will always be in doubt. Without your full commitment to this cause, the kingdom will not be bound."

"Then I will put my hand to it, my lord," Lancelot said. "Because you require it, not because I desire it." He shuttered his eyes.

"Do not just put your hand there. You must *try,* damn you," the King whispered fiercely. "You must really try."

Lancelot opened his eyes and some small fire, reflecting perhaps from the candles or the torches or the solstice flames, seemed to glow there for a moment. Then, in an instant, the fire in his eyes was gone. He stepped up to the stone, put his hand to the sword, and seemed to address it. His lips moved but no sound came out. Taking a deep breath, he pulled. Then, letting the breath out slowly, he leaned back.

The stone began to move.

The crowd gasped in a single voice.

"Arthur . . ." Kai began, his hand on the King's arm.

Sweat appeared on Lancelot's brow and the King could feel an answering band of sweat on his own. He could feel the weight of Lancelot's pull between his own shoulder blades and he held his breath with the knight.

The stone began to slide along the courtyard mosaic, but the sword did not slip from its mooring. It was a handle for the stone, nothing more. After a few inches, the stone stopped moving.

Lancelot withdrew his hand from the hilt, bowed slightly toward the King, and took two steps back.

"I cannot unsheath the King's sword," he said. His voice was remarkably level for a man who had just moved a ton of stone.

"Is there no one else?" asked Merlinnus, slowly looking around.

No one in the crowd dared to meet his eyes and there followed a long, full silence.

Then, from the left, came a familiar light voice. "Let King Arthur try." It was Gawen.

At once the crowd picked up its cue. "Arthur! Arthur! Arthur!" they shouted.

Wading into their noise like a swimmer in heavy swells breasting the waves, the King walked to the stone. Putting his right hand on the sword hilt, he turned his face to the people.

"For Britain!" he cried.

Merlinnus nodded, crossed his forefingers, and sighed a spell in Latin.

Arthur pulled. With a slight *whoosh* the sword slid out of the slot. He put his left hand above his right on the hilt and swung the sword over his head once, twice, and then a third time. Then he brought it slowly down before him until its point touched the earth.

"Now I be king. Of *all* Britain," he said.

Kai picked up the circlet from the stone and placed it on Arthur's head, and the chant of his name began anew. But even as he was swept up, up, up into the air by Kai and Lancelot, to ride their shoulders above the crowd, Arthur's eyes met the mage's. He whispered fiercely to Merlinnus, who could read his lips though his voice could scarcely carry against the noise.

"I will see you in your tower. Tonight!"

Merlinnus was waiting when, two hours later, the King slipped into his room, the sword in his left hand.

"So now you are king of all Britain indeed," said Merlinnus. "And none can say you no. Was I not right? A bit of legerdemain and . . ."

The king's face was grey in the room's candlelight.

"Merlinnus, you do not understand. I am *not* the king. There is another."

"Another what?" asked the mage.

"Another king. Another sword."

Merlinnus shook his head. "You are tired, lord. It has been a long day and an even longer night."

Arthur came over and grabbed the old man's shoulder with his right hand. "Merlinnus, *this* is *not the same sword.*"

"My lord, you are mistaken. It can be no other."

Arthur swept the small crown off his head and dropped it into the mage's lap. "I am a simple man, Merlinnus, and I am an honest one. I do not know much, though I am trying to learn more. I read slowly and understand only with help. What I am best at is soldiering. What I know best is swords. The sword I held months ago in my hands is not the sword I hold now. That sword had a balance to it, a grace such as I had never felt before. It knew me, knew my hand. There was a pattern on the blade that looked now like wind, now like fire. This blade, though it has fine watering, looks like nothing.

"I am not an imaginative man, Merlinnus, so I am not imagining this. This is not the sword that was in the stone. And if it is not, where is that sword? And what man took it? For he, not I, is the rightful born king of all Britain. And I would be the first in the land to bend my knee to him."

Merlinnus put his hand to his head and stared at the crown in his lap. "I swear to you, Arthur, no man alive could move that sword from the stone lest I spoke the words."

There was a slight sound from behind the heavy curtains bordering the window, and a small figure emerged holding a sword in two hands.

"I am afraid that I took the sword, my lords."

"Gawen!" cried Merlinnus and Arthur at once.

The boy knelt before Arthur and held up the sword before him.

Arthur bent down and pulled the boy up. The sword was between them.

"It is I should kneel to you, my young king."

Gawen shook his head and a slight flush covered his cheeks. "I cannot be king now or ever. Not *rex quondam, rex que futurus.*"

"How pulled you the sword, then?" Merlinnus asked. "Speak. Be quick about it."

The boy placed the sword in Arthur's hands. "I brought a slab of butter to the stone one night and melted the butter over candle flames. When it was a river of gold I poured it into the slot and the sword slid out. Just like that."

"A trick. A homey trick that any herb wife might . . ." Merlinnus began.

Arthur turned on him, sadly. "No more a trick, mage, than my pulling a sword loosed by your spell. The boy is, in fact, the better of us two, for he worked it out by himself." He shifted and spoke directly to Gawen. "A king needs such cunning. But he needs a good right hand as well. I shall be yours, my lord, though I envy you the sword."

"The sword is yours, Arthur, never mine. Though I can now thrust and slash, having learned that much under the ham-handedness of your good tutor, I shall not ride to war. I have learned to fear the blade's edge as well as respect it." Gawen smiled.

The King turned again to Merlinnus. "Help me, mage. I do not understand."

Merlinnus rose and put the crown back on Arthur's head. "But I think I do, at last, though why I should be so slow to note it, I wonder. Age must dull the mind as well as the fingers. I have had an ague of the brain this fall. I said no man but you could pull the sword—and no *man* has." He held out his hand. "Come, child. You shall make a lovely May Queen, I think. By then the hair should be long enough for Sir Kai's list. Though what we shall ever do about the short utterances is beyond me."

"A *girl?* He's a girl?" Arthur looked baffled.

"Magic even beyond my making," said Merlinnus. "But what is your name, child? Surely not Gawen."

"Guenevere," she said. "I came to learn to be a knight in order to challenge Sir Gawain, who dishonored my sister. But I find—"

"That he is a bubblehead and not worth the effort?" interrupted Arthur. "He shall marry her *and* he shall be glad of it, for you shall be my queen and, married to your sister, he shall be my brother."

Guenevere laughed. "She will like that, too. Her head is as empty as his. But she *is* my sister. And she still loves him. Without a brother to champion her, I had to do."

Merlinnus laughed. "And you did splendidly. But about that butter trick . . ."

Guenevere put her hand over her breast. "I shall never tell as long as . . ." She hesitated.

"Anything," Arthur said. "Ask for anything."

"As long as I can have my sword back."

Arthur looked longingly at the sword, hefted it once, and then put it solemnly in her hand.

"Oh, not *this* one," Guenevere said. "It is too heavy and unwieldy. It does not sit well in my hand. I mean the other, the one that *you* pulled."

"Oh, *that,*" said Arthur. "With all my heart."

THE SEA MAN

CHAPTER ONE

The sky over the sea is a deep blue slate.

"And neither bird nor cloud dares write upon it, my darling daughter, Jannie," Lieutenant Huiskemp writes in his careful script. "But there are always wonders below the water. Not magic, dear one. Just things we do not know yet. But once seen and examined, these wonders can be explained."

He draws tiny dolphins and flying fish in the margins of his letter. They leap from line to line, a strange punctuation. "I send you kisses, safe and snug in Zeeland. And kisses, too, for your dear mama. You must be a good girl and not cry when she combs your hair or complain over much when she plaits it. Your loving father, Maarten Huiskemp, April 1663."

He looks out across the water to the shore. There the mills spin the heavy wind in their long arms. Cattle graze the dike grasses. Along the roadside, thousands of colored tulips bow and bend with every passing breeze.

Lieutenant Huiskemp smiles, stands, and stretches. The wind puzzles through his yellow hair. He is a tall man, his legs like a stork's, long and bony. He towers above the men in his crew. When he sits down again, he draws a whale at the bottom of the letter spouting Jannie's name. Then he draws a portrait of Jannie herself, brown braids standing out stiff to each side. He adds a fish tail instead of legs, so that she looks as if she is swimming next to the whale.

Though he does not believe mermaids are real, never having seen any, the lieutenant knows Jannie will like the pictures. She loves the fairy stories he reads to her and soon enough she will have to give up such childish things. Besides, it is the last letter he can send her for a long time. Presently his ship, *The Water Nix,* bobbing at anchor off the coast, must join the fleet in the open sea.

There is a sound behind him and the lieutenant turns quickly. It is the young cabin boy, Pieter, just newly come aboard. He has yet to learn their quiet ways.

"Do you want some tea, sir?" Pieter asks. His voice still holds the word in awe, for tea is something only the captain and the lieutenant are allowed, it being a rare and expensive drink.

"No, son," Lieutenant Huiskemp says. "But you can tell me what you think of this." He holds the letter up.

The breeze makes it ripple like the sea.

"I cannot read it, sir," Pieter says, brushing the fair hair from his eyes.

The lieutenant catches hold of the end and pulls the letter tight against the wind.

"I mean, I cannot read, sir," Pieter says. There is fresh color in his cheeks.

"Neither can my little girl, Jannie," the lieutenant says quickly. "That is why I draw pictures for her. Surely . . ." He chuckles, and it is a comforting sound. "Surely you can read them."

Pieter smiles shyly. "I can read pictures, sir." Leaning over to look at the letter, his hands carefully behind him, he says: "Why, it is a sperm whale, I think, sir. And a *zee wyven,* a mermaid, there at the bottom. My father saw one once."

"A whale?" the lieutenant asks.

"A mermaid," Pieter says seriously.

"Did he?" The lieutenant keeps a straight face. He will not laugh at Pieter. He respects all his men, and this one is young enough to learn the difference between science and stories. But not, the lieutenant feels, by means of laughter.

"He saw it at a fair," Pieter answers.

"Do not believe everything you see at a fair," the lieutenant says, matching Pieter in seriousness. "Sometimes it is nothing more than a trick of mirrors and smoke that men play to steal your coins. Or a monkey's head sewn to the tail of a carp. To fool the gullible."

"I will remember that, sir," Pieter says. But he does not sound quite convinced.

"Good boy." Lieutenant Huiskemp dismisses Pieter with a nod and bends back to his letter. This time he writes to his wife, but there are no fancies in it. It is about the weather and the waywardness of man.

CHAPTER TWO

The sky has not changed the whole of the day. Except for birds scripting across its empty slate, the sky is the same.

Aboard *The Water Nix,* it has been a day of preparations. The busy sailors scrub and rub and polish the ship, getting it ready for its voyage out to the open sea. By early evening, the sky has darkened overhead, but otherwise has not changed.

Lieutenant Huiskemp is once again on deck. This time Pieter is quieter in his approach, but still the lieutenant hears him. He turns and looks sternly at the boy, setting down the spyglass with which he has been checking the shore.

"Do you want something to eat, sir?" Pieter asks.

Just as the lieutenant is about to answer, there is a shout from one of the sailors. It shatters the peace of the ship.

"Look! Look!"

Huiskemp shades his eyes against the sun so low on

the horizon. He walks on his stork legs to the other side of the ship. Pieter follows behind, like a shadow.

The men are boiling around the railing, jostling one another. They are pointing out to the open sea.

The lieutenant sees an odd whirling in the water, as if it were pleated like a piece of cloth. He has never seen anything like it before. "What is going on?" he asks.

"Something horrible!" shouts one of the sailors, his eyes never leaving the troubled waters.

The lieutenant is not one for fast judgments, though he is one for quick actions. With his spyglass he watches where the water is roiling.

Suddenly a hand rises out of the water, then an arm, two arms, a man's head. It looks as if the man is praying or shouting for help, but oddly he makes no sound.

"Sir, he is drowning," Pieter cries.

"Lower a boat at once," the lieutenant commands. He does not take the spyglass from his eye.

A sailor named Henk and two others, Hans and Wilhelm, are lowered in the rescue boat and they row over the troubled sea. Along the railing, the other sailors call out instructions. Only the lieutenant and Pieter are silent, the one because he knows the men and trusts them; the other, who is too new for trust, because he does not.

The strange pleated waves never trouble *The Water Nix,* but they do rock the little rescue boat, so much that Hans and Wilhelm must hold on to the sides to keep from falling out. Only Henk, his hands on the oars, seems oblivious to the motion. The muscles on his arms bunch and pleat much like the sea as he rows.

When the rescue boat reaches the man, Wilhelm frantically signals back to the ship. Hans shouts something, but it is carried away by the wind. They bend over the side and struggle to lift the man into the boat.

The lieutenant can see he is tangled in netting. He has broad, muscular shoulders and dark curly hair glinting green, like phosphorescence.

"Like a Portugee," whispers Pieter.

The lieutenant glares at him and Pieter is suddenly silenced, recalling that he has been lectured before about saying such things.

When the man is halfway into the boat, everyone can see that he is not entirely a man! From the waist up he is as human as the sailors. But below the waist, he is a fish, with a tail like a tunny's, the scales all silver and blue and the water beading off them like jewels.

The lieutenant lowers his spyglass, but even without it he can see the tail. Still he will not let himself believe.

In the boat, Hans and Wilhelm try to push the creature back into the water. Henk takes one oar from the oarlock, prepared to beat the sea man into submission.

Recalled to his duty, Lieutenant Huiskemp picks up a speaking trumpet and shouts through it. "Bring that . . . thing . . . on board. Bring it on board." He is quite suddenly excited. And he is puzzled. *It is a mystery,* he reminds himself. *And once examined . . .*

Being good sailors, Henk and Hans and Wilhelm obey, though first they wrap the sea man more securely in the net. Then, staying as far away from the creature as they dare, they row it back to the ship.

"But why, sir?" asks young Pieter. "Why bring the thing on board?"

The question is one the lieutenant asks himself as quickly, so he does not reprimand the boy for asking. But he mumbles out the only answer he can find. "In the interests of science, lad. The captain will want to have a look at it when he returns." He adds to himself in sober contemplation, *As do I. As do I.*

CHAPTER THREE

The slate of the sky is a strange orange and gray now, orange from the setting sun, gray around the edges, as night creeps in.

When the sea man is drawn up on the deck, tangled in netting, the sailors crowd around for a good look. Up close, the sea man looks more and more like a fish. There are webbings as gray as storm air between its fingers. Its mouth is round like a fish's; its eyes a pale, watery blue. There are gray-green hairs curling on its chest in the pattern of seashells. It has red gill slits along its neck. It lies gray and gasping on the deck and does not speak.

"What a hideous thing," says Hans. He looks at the sea man from the safety of nearly five feet away. Having touched it once, he does not want to have to do so again.

The sea man suddenly slaps its tail against the deck and all the men jump back. The sound is as loud as a cannon shot.

"That is bad luck," Henk says, smoothing his fair moustache. "We should kill it."

"We should sell it," says Wilhelm. The others agree. They argue about prices while the sea man gasps.

"Sell it?" asks Pieter. "Sell it where? To a fair? My father saw a *zee wyven* once at a fair. But it was much smaller, he said. About the size of a carp."

"Sell it to the university professors in Leyden," says Wilhelm. "They would give many guilders to study it."

Slap. Slap. The tail against the deck is not so loud now.

"Bad luck," Henk repeats. He spits in the sea man's direction.

"University professors do not care about luck," says Wilhelm.

Henk spits again. "All men care about luck."

The sea man wriggles along the deck but still makes no sound, except for the *slap-slap* of its tail. Its round mouth opens and closes soundlessly.

The lieutenant is equally silent. For a moment he feels as if he is drowning in a dream.

Henk leans over. "Phew. And it smells."

Another sailor laughs, but not heartily. "Like a fish."

Wilhelm slaps his thigh. "Like a Portu—"

The lieutenant opens his mouth, interrupts. "What would you have it smell like? It *is* a fish. It only looks, in this light, like a man."

"Such things are bad luck," Henk repeats. "We should kill it quickly and *then* sell it to the professors. They will not care if it is alive or dead. It is bad luck, I tell you. I felt it when I put my hand on its back. The bad luck came right through my fingers." He holds up his right hand as if the print of the luck might be seen. His other hand reaches for the knife at his belt.

"No knives, man," the lieutenant says, "or I will put you in irons in the hold."

All this time the sea man has been silent, though its mouth opens and closes, opens and closes.

"Is it deaf, sir?" asks Pieter, talking to the lieutenant. "I have an uncle in Haarlem who is deaf. He does not make a sound, either." Without waiting for an answer, the boy kneels down by the sea man and puts his hand on the creature's shoulder. He shouts into its shell-like ear. He seems absolutely unafraid, as if his youth confers on him some kind of immortality. "Are you deaf?"

At the shout, the sea man's eyes open wide. Its head jerks back. Its arms, still bound to its side by the netting, move as much as they can. The right hand is partially clear of the net, and the fingers wriggle slightly; the webbing between wobbles.

Pieter turns his head and looks at the lieutenant, his hand still on the creature's bare gray shoulder. "Not deaf, then, sir." He stands up and moves back, away from the sea man who is once again still. Pieter does not, even once, wipe his hand on his shirt.

The sailors break their tight circle around the sea man and look somewhat ashamed, all except Henk, whose face has grown dark, like the sky.

"About your work, men," says the lieutenant. And they go, though they still manage to keep an eye on the creature. The lieutenant, however, kneels down beside it. He speaks to it in Dutch, then Danish, German, and English. He speaks slowly, as if to a child or to a simpleton. He tries French. At last he says a few words in Portuguese.

The sea man opens its mouth again. This close, the lieutenant can see that its mouth is hollow. Like a fish, it has teeth, but no tongue. "Of course you cannot talk," the lieutenant murmurs. Only Pieter—and the sea man—hear him.

At the lieutenant's voice, this time the sea man tries to sit up.

"Who are you?" the lieutenant asks in Dutch. "*What* are you?" he asks, even more slowly. He points at the sea man when he says this and draws a question mark between them with his finger.

The sea man sits all the way up, watching the lieutenant's fingers with its watery eyes. Some of the netting is draped over its hunched shoulders like a shawl, so it looks like an old man. A gray old man. The fingers on its one free hand wave quickly, like seaweed in a heavy swell. *Like a semaphore,* the lieutenant thinks. It is not a comfortable thought.

"Careful," Henk calls from his place far back on the deck. Even in the quickening dark, he has seen the movement. "It is dangerous. Surely its bite is full of poison."

"Give me your knife," the lieutenant says at last, holding out his hand. "Quickly, man."

Henk runs forward and hands him the knife. "Fillet it," he says. "It will make a big stew."

CHAPTER FOUR

A solitary gull writes a warning on the sky slate, then dives down into the sea. No one sees it. They are all intent on the knife in the lieutenant's hand. They are as silent as the sea man.

Lieutenant Huiskemp slices through the netting, entirely freeing the sea man's hands and forearms. The sea man flexes its left fingers, then the right, and the sailors freeze for a moment, as if the flexing fingers have enchanted them.

Suddenly the sea man makes rapid, strange signs with both its hands, right and left crossing in complicated patterns. The webbings between the fingers pulse green and pink and gray. Then the right hand reaches for the lieutenant's knife.

Grabbing his own knife, Wilhelm lurches forward. "Look out!" he cries. And adds as an afterthought, "Sir!"

"Stop, man!" The lieutenant holds up the hand with the knife, stopping Wilhelm in his tracks. With his other hand, the lieutenant takes hold of the sea man's fingers. They are slippery and wet and cold. They tap out some kind of message in the lieutenant's palm, but though the lieutenant knows many languages, this is not one of them. *Still,* he thinks, *only humans have language.*

He drops the creature's hand and turns to the men. "A fish is not dangerous out of the water. Come, help me with this thing. . . ."

The sailors look at him strangely. One even crosses himself. The others back away.

"Touch it again, sir?" Henk asks. "We are not crazy. Not like the boy."

Lieutenant Huiskemp says, "Captain Van Tassel will be back tonight with our orders. He will want to see this creature alive. Until then, we will keep it safe in the hold." He puts a hand on Pieter's shoulder and says to the men, "Only this boy has shown any real courage."

At that the men grumble, and Hans reminds them all that he and Wilhelm and Henk have already done their share. So three others, mouths set in a way to indicate they have found their own courage, pick up the sea man; but their eyes, frightened, give them away. They carry the creature—one by the shoulders, two at the tail—to the hold door, which Henk pulls open. There they heave the sea man once, twice, and throw it in.

It lands with a loud *thunk* and, after a moment, they hear another noise. The creature is whistling. The sound is soft and mournful.

"A sea song?" Hans asks.

"A dirge," the lieutenant whispers. He knows that whales can sing. And wolves. He knows that birds can whistle. "A dirge."

Only young Pieter hears him.

CHAPTER FIVE

The sky's slate is now a soft night blue. Only one star is out, like punctuation to a sentence yet to be written.

In his cabin, the lieutenant has eaten dinner alone and thinks about the sea man. Since he has seen it, since he has touched it, he must believe it is real. A sea man in the flesh, not in the imagination.

"But a sea man is not really a man," he tells himself. He sets out his argument carefully. "It is a creature of the ocean, of the deep. An animal. A fish. We have not yet explored all that is below. This creature is a mystery. But it is not magic. Science will, in the end, explain all." Still, he is uncomfortable with his reasoning and does not know why, so he turns his thoughts to the sea man in the hold. He wonders how long it can live there, away from the ministrations of the sea.

He stands and paces his cabin once, then twice. *A fish,* he reminds himself, *dies out of the water.* He is decided. He will check on it and, in the interests of science, give it what it needs.

The men on the deck are clustered about the forecastle, talking in whispers. The lieutenant says nothing to them but goes directly to the dark hold. He lights a lantern, raises it high. The sea man looks up at the light with clouded eyes. It waves a feeble hand.

Leaving the light, the lieutenant goes up on deck, fills a bucket with seawater, and carries it down again. Even when he douses the sea man with the water, the creature scarcely moves.

For a moment, a long moment, they stare at each other in silence. There is something compelling about the creature, mesmerizing, but not evil. *Henk is wrong about that.*

"Are you . . ." the lieutenant begins. "Do you . . ." Then he stops entirely and shakes his head. "You are a creature," he says. "And understand no more than my wife's dog, Tulip."

The sea man makes no answer.

Taking the lantern with him, Lieutenant Huiskemp goes up the stairs once more. The air above is suddenly cool and fresh smelling. He breathes it in gratefully, then sighs.

Young Pieter is standing at the railing, looking out across the dark ocean. The sky is now fully lit by a round moon and flickering stars.

"The captain did not come back with the evening tide," Pieter says.

"Then he will come in the morning," the lieutenant answers. He is not sure the creature will be alive then, but he does not say this to Pieter.

"Sir, Henk is telling stories about sea dragons and kraken and the vengeance of the mer," Pieter says. His voice trembles and he sounds, suddenly, very young. A child. "He says they are all evil. That they are satanic. That they have no souls."

The lieutenant nods solemnly. He can hear Henk's voice now, coming through the breezeless dark. Henk is a strong storyteller and the sea makes believers of all men. Lieutenant Huiskemp worries about the dying creature in the hold; about Henk, who is rousing the sailors; about the trembling boy at his side.

"Do you believe so, sir?" Pieter asks.

The lieutenant startles, then turns his head toward the boy. "Believe what, son?"

"That the sea man has no soul."

"It is one of God's own creatures," he says slowly. "And as such, we must love it. But the only one with a soul, so Scripture tells us, is man. It is what distinguishes us from animals." He pauses. "And from fish." He does not tell Pieter that it is *language* that truly distinguishes humankind from the lower orders. Science and religion are too heady a mix for this unlettered boy.

"But what of the story of the water nix, sir?" Pieter asks.

"The story of our boat?" For a moment the lieutenant is confused.

"No," Pieter says. "It is an old tale my father told me. He said there was once a priest who met a water nix who begged and begged him to baptize her. But he refused, saying that as she was a water sprite, she had no soul. He told her, 'Sooner would my old walking stick sprout leaves than a nix shall have a soul.' And even as he spoke, green furled from the stick: stems and vines and leaves." Pieter takes a deep breath. "Is that true, sir? I mean, how could it be, if what Henk says is true?"

"It is a story," the lieutenant says.

"But is it *true*?" the boy asks, the tremor back in his voice.

The lieutenant is about to say *What is truth?* when the boy grabs his sleeve.

"Sir—look!" He points to the water. In the moon's light, the boy's hair is silvery and hardly seems real. "There is something in the water."

"There are dolphins," Lieutenant Huiskemp says, suddenly tired of the whole thing; of the distinction between what is real and what is true. He wishes to be far away, either at sea or on the shore. *In between,* he realizes, *is the most difficult of all places to be.* Like being a lieutenant but not captain; like being on board a ship; like being a boy among men; like being a lettered man with an unlettered crew.

"There are whales," he adds. But still he looks to where Pieter is pointing and sees that there is, indeed, something odd there, though he cannot see it clearly. "Night," he says to the boy, "makes many things seem unnatural." But the tremor is now in his own voice.

Pieter turns to him and, in a voice made old by truth, declares, "There is a sea man in our hold and we pulled it in by day. You told me such things were tricks to get coins. Yet there he is, half man and half fish."

Half man and half fish, the lieutenant thinks. *Someone else who is in between.* He speaks quickly, as if truth can be made by running words together. "What is in the hold is a fish, not a man." He wishes he could believe that entirely. Or believe otherwise. "And it is dying out of the sea."

"Dying?" There is a world of sorrow in the boy's one word. It shames Huiskemp to his very soul. Then the boy grabs his sleeve once more. "Sir—that *something* in the sea. It is nearer still."

The lieutenant is forced to look more closely by his fear, by his hope, by the truth.

The sea, below the slate of sky, is strangely pleated once again.

CHAPTER SIX

The sentences written on the night's slate are these: full moon, a thousand stars, and the thinnest wisp of a cloud, like a hyphen, against the moon. Something dark and light is reflected in the sea.

"Quick, my boy," whispers the lieutenant, suddenly decided, "you and I will haul that creature on deck. Soul or no soul, perhaps this time it will speak to us in a way we can understand. Perhaps it can tell us what is down there, swimming by our ship's bow. Perhaps it knows if that thing down there means us any harm. I am in charge while the captain is away and I must guard the ship."

"What of the men, sir? Shouldn't they help?"

"They are captives of Henk's story, lad. At night a tale has more command than any officer."

"I understand, sir," Pieter says. And the lieutenant is sure he does.

They hurry below. The smell in the hold is stronger now. It is a dark smell, and damp. It is redolent of decay. When Pieter lights the lantern, they see the sea man humped in a corner. It flings one green-gray arm across its eyes to shield them from the light, except it moves in slow motion, as if swimming. Its breath is labored, its gill slits now all gray.

"I will take the shoulders," says the lieutenant. "You carry the tail. We will move it to the stern, away from Henk and his stories."

They struggle with the sea man, who lies limp and heavy in their arms. Its skin is no longer slippery, no longer wet, but feels spongy and warm. Twice Pieter drops the tail on the stairs and it slaps against the steps, a loud thudding. The lieutenant breathes his worry through his teeth, a soft, nervous whistle. At the sound, the sea man tries to twist in the lieutenant's arms. It manages to look up in his face, but they are so far from the lantern's light, they are just two shadows in the dark. And in the dark, their faces are the same.

At last the lieutenant and Pieter wrestle the sea man onto the deck, near the starboard railing. They set it down and it breathes deeply for several long moments, as if gathering strength from the salt air. Then, hardly moving, it purses its lips and sends out a strange, frothy whistle. For a long while everything seems to still: the rocking ship, the hearty wind, the rolling waves, the sound of Henk's voice from the forecastle.

Then there is a sudden answer from the sea: a long, high, full whistle, ornamented with sweet flutings. The sea man sits up. It begins to thrash and twist, humping and thumping against the railing. As it moves, its tired, dying whistle gains energy, changing to a stretched sad note, as loud and lowing as a foghorn.

The water below the boat grows more pleated still and *The Water Nix* bobs frantically at anchor. Henk's startled voice cries out in the dark. The other men echo him, like leader and chorus of a badly sung song.

Pieter and the lieutenant lean over the railing and stare at the pleated sea. Below them in the water is a figure outlined in moonlight. It has long, green curling hair. It has softly rounded breasts. It has a child in its arms. The child has a tail like an upside-down question mark and two green braids standing stiffly to either side.

"Lieutenant, look! A *zee wyven*," says Pieter.

"A sea wife," the lieutenant whispers, staring. "She has braided her daughter's hair." His voice is as awed as Pieter's, and by this one simple fact. "She has plaited it into two braids." At last he is a believer, science and story coming together.

At the sound of their voices, the child turns in her mother's arms. She puts her head back and the moon lights her face fully. She is laughing, but silently. Her little tail strokes the water. The sea wife's face shows no such delight. Drops of *water—Tears?* the lieutenant wonders—cascade down her cheeks.

Without a word, Lieutenant Huiskemp kneels by the sea man's side. Using his bare hands, he rips away the last of the netting from the sea man's shoulders, though he rips his own skin in the process. The blood drops, black, onto the sea man's skin. He seems to feel it and looks, briefly, into the lieutenant's eyes.

Huiskemp picks up the sea man and, staggering under the weight, hoists him upright against the railing.

"This is for my own little Jannie," he says. "And for the nix." He does not know himself if he means Pieter's story or the ship.

Pieter stoops down and, silently, gathers up the sea man's tail.

Just then, Henk and the other men move forward. There is a long silence, broken only by the sound of the waves against the hull. The men all stare at the quieted sea, Pieter holding the sea man's arm. It aches, but not more than his heart at the sea man's going.

"Well," Wilhelm says at last, "there is one curiosity the professors will not get to study."

"Nor will we see any money," says Hans.

"Mark me, he will send evil," Henk says. But no one listens to him.

Lieutenant Huiskemp smiles. "We will not see the sea man again." He turns and gestures with his right hand. The bleeding has stopped. "This deck is a great mess. I want it shipshape before Captain Van Tassel returns on the morning tide."

And as it is no more than an ordinary command, the sailors thankfully move to their tasks.

CHAPTER SEVEN

But the lieutenant is wrong. When they set sail, for three nights running, under a clean slate of sky, the sea man surfaces again, surrounded by pleated water. He does not whistle, but his hands move quick and slow, quick and slow.

The lieutenant, who learns languages easily, learns to read those fingers. And he learns to speak the same way.

The first night the lieutenant picks up counting and grammar. He learns greetings, and the names of many things: water, fish, ship, bird, sky. The sea man teaches him the seven ways of describing waves and the thirteen terms for whale. There are separate names for "*zee wyven*" and "land wife;" but the lieutenant is surprised to find that the word for "child" is the same.

The second night the two men exchange bits of history, which, like most family stories, are made up of equal parts of truth and of lies. On that second eve, the lieutenant speaks of life aboard ship, of the unlettered men who can still read their routes in the writing of the stars. His slow fingers tell the sea man how he, a Haarlem lad, trained to science and mathematics, came by slow, sure steps to the sea. His fingers stumble, trying to find words for "science" and "mathematics." The sea man, of course, has none. At last the lieutenant settles on gestures that show something being built up, bigger and bigger. Perhaps "creation" is what he has signed. Then he gestures finger added to finger, for "counting." The sea man seems to understand.

On the second night, they also speak of their homes. Huiskemp's hands talk of his Portuguese wife and his own dark-haired daughter, so like the sea man's own child. He outlines Jannie's braids against his own head, threading his fingers till they both laugh at the tangles. The lieutenant laughs out loud, a hearty sound, and the sea man laughs silently, his mouth full of bubbles. When the lieutenant is done, his hands ache, as one's ears ache after a long night of conversation with a friend.

But on the third night out at sea, the sea man does not come with stories. He comes instead with a warning. He rises, whistling for attention, and then, hands and fingers frantic, he spells out wild waves, lightning, storms.

Patiently, the lieutenant translates for Captain Van Tassel and the crew. Even Henk is convinced. The captain orders them back to harbor, where they ride out the storm.

"And it was only the sea man's warnings," the lieutenant writes to Jannie at the bottom of the page, "that brought us safe to our mooring in view of the waving tulips and the windmills with the storms in their long arms. Only our ship was undamaged when so many others were battered and broken or lost at sea."

He decorates the envelope with a picture of the sea man and the sea wife and their little sea girl, who—except for the gray webbings between her fingers, except for the question-mark tail—looks remarkably like little Jannie Huiskemp, so safe upon the shore in a snug little home in Zeeland.

MEMOIRS OF A BOTTLE DJINN

The sea was as dark as old blood, not the wine color poets sing of. In the early evening it seemed to stain the sand.

As usual for this time of year, the air was heavy, ill-omened.

I walked out onto the beach below my master's house whenever I could slip away unnoticed, though it was a dangerous practice. Still, it was one necessary to my well-being. I had been a sailor for many more years than I had been a slave, and the smell of the salt air was not a luxury for me but a necessity.

If a seabird had washed up dead at my feet, its belly would have contained black worms and other evil auguries, so dark and lowering was the sky. So I wondered little at the bottle that the sea had deposited before me, certain it contained noxious fumes at best, the legacy of its long cradling in such a salty womb.

In my country poets sing the praises of wine and gift its color to the water along the shores of Hellas, and I can think of no finer hymn. But in this land they believe their prophet forbade them strong drink. They are a sober race who reward themselves in heaven even as they deny themselves on earth. It is a system of which I do not approve, but then I am a Greek by birth and a heathen by inclination, despite my master's long importuning. It is only by chance that I have not yet lost an eye, an ear, or a hand to my master's unforgiving code. He finds me amusing, but it has been seven years since I have had a drink.

I stared at the bottle. If I had any luck at all, the bottle had fallen from a foreign ship and its contents would still be potable. But then, if I had any luck at all, I would not be a slave in Arabia, a Greek sailor washed up on these shores, the same as the bottle at my feet. My father, who was a cynic like his father before him, left me with a cynic's name—Antithias—a wry heart, and an acid tongue, none proper legacies for a slave.

But as blind Homer wrote, "Few sons are like their father; many are worse." I guessed that the wine, if drinkable, would come from an inferior year. And with that thought, I bent to pick it up.

The glass was a cloudy green, like the sea after a violent storm. Like the storm that had wrecked my ship and cast me onto a slaver's shore. There were darker flecks along the bottom, a sediment that surely foretold an undrinkable wine. I let the bottle warm between my palms.

Since the glass was too dark to let me see more, I waited past my first desire and was well into my second, letting it rise up in me like the heat of passion. The body has its own memories, though I must be frank: passion, like wine, was simply a fragrance remembered. Slaves are not lent the services of concubines, nor was one my age and race useful for breeding. It had only been by feigning impotence that I had kept that part of my anatomy intact—another of my master's unforgiving laws. Even in the dark of night, alone on my pallet, I forwent the pleasures of the hand, for there were spies everywhere in his house and the eunuchs were a notably gossipy lot. Little but a slave's tongue lauding morality stood between gossip and scandal, stood between me and the knife. Besides, the women of Arabia tempted me little. They were like the bottle in my hand—beautiful and empty. A wind blowing across the mouth of each could make them sing, but the tunes were worth little. I liked my women like my wine—full-bodied and tanged with history, bringing a man into poetry. So I had put my passion into work these past seven years, slave's work though it was. Blind Homer had it right, as usual: "Labor conquers all things." Even old lusts for women and wine.

Philosophy did not conquer movement, however, and my hand found the cork of the bottle before I could stay it. With one swift movement I had plucked the stopper out. A thin strand of smoke rose into the air. A very bad year indeed, I thought, as the cork crumbled in my hand.

Up and up and up the smoky rope ascended and I, bottle in hand, could not move, such was my disappointment. Even my father's cynicism and his father's before him had not prepared me for such a sudden loss of all hope. My mind, a moment before full of anticipation and philosophy, was now in blackest despair. I found myself without will, reliving in my mind the moment of my capture and the first bleak days of my enslavement.

That is why it was several minutes before I realized that the smoke had begun to assume a recognizable shape above the bottle's gaping mouth: long, sensuous legs glimpsed through diaphanous trousers; a waist my hands could easily span; breasts beneath a short embroidered cotton vest as round as ripe pomegranates; and a face . . . a face that was smoke and air. I remembered suddenly a girl in the port of Alexandria who sold fruit from a basket and gave me a smile. She was the last girl who had smiled upon me when I was a free man and I, not knowing the future, had ignored her, so intent was I on my work. My eyes clouded over at the memory, and when they were clear again, I saw that same smile imprinted upon the face of the djinn.

"I am what you would have me be, Master," her low voice called down to me.

I reached up a hand to help her step to earth, but my

hand went through hers, mortal flesh through smoky air. It was then, I think, that I really believed she was what I guessed her to be.

She smiled. "What is your wish, Master?"

I took the time to smile back. "How many wishes do I get?"

She shook her head but still she smiled, that Alexandrian smile, all lips without a hint of teeth. But there was a dimple in her left cheek. "One, my master, for you drew the cork but once."

"And if I draw it again?"

"The cork is gone." This time her teeth showed, as did a second dimple, on the right.

I sighed and looked at the crumbled mess in my hand, then sprinkled the cork like seed upon the sand. "Just one."

"Does a slave need more?" she asked in that same low voice.

"You mean that I should ask for my freedom?" I laughed and sat down on the sand. The little waves that outran the big ones tickled my feet, for I had come out barefoot. I looked across the water. "Free to be a sailor again at my age? Free to let the sun peel the skin from my back, free to heave my guts over the stern in a blinding rain, free to wreck once more upon a slaver's shore?"

She drifted down beside me and, though her smoky hand could not hold mine, I felt a breeze across my palm that could have been her touch. I could see through her to the cockleshell and white stones pocking the sand.

"Free to make love to Alexandrian women," she said. "Free to drink strong wine."

"Free to have regrets in the morning either way," I replied. Then I laughed.

She laughed back. "What about the freedom to indulge in a dinner of roast partridge in lemons and eggplant? What about hard-boiled eggs sprinkled with vermilion? What about cinnamon tripes?" It was the meal my master had just had.

"Rich food like rich women gives me heartburn," I said.

"The freedom to fill your pockets with coins?"

Looking away from her, over the clotted sea, I whispered to myself, "'Accursed thirst for gold! What dost thou not compel mortals to do,'" a line from the *Aeneid.*

"Virgil was a wise man," she said quietly. "For a Roman!" Then she laughed.

I turned to look at her closely for the first time. A woman who knows Virgil, be she djinn or mortal, was a woman to behold. Though her body was still composed of that shifting, smoky air, the features on her face now held steady. She no longer looked like the Alexandrian girl, but had a far more sophisticated beauty. Lined with kohl, her eyes were gray as smoke and her hair the same color. There were shadows along her cheeks that emphasized the bone, and faint smile lines crinkling the skin at each corner of her generous mouth. She was not as young as she had first appeared, but then I was not so young myself.

"Ah, Antithias," she said, smiling at me, "even djinns

age, though corked up in a bottle slows down the process immeasurably."

I spoke Homer's words to her then: "'In youth and beauty, wisdom is but rare.'" I added in my own cynic's way, "If ever."

"You think me *wise,* then?" she asked, then laughed, and her laughter was like the tinkling of camel bells. "But a gaudy parrot is surely as wise, reciting another's words as his own."

"I know no parrots who hold Virgil and Homer in their mouths," I said, gazing at her not with longing but with a kind of wonder. "No djinn either."

"You know many?"

"Parrots, yes; djinn, no. You are my first."

"Then you are lucky, indeed, Greek, that you called up one of the worshipers of Allah and not one of the followers of Iblis."

I nodded. "Lucky, indeed."

"So, to your wish, Master," she said.

"You call me Master, I who am a slave," I said. "Do *you* not want the freedom you keep offering me? Freedom from the confining green bottle, freedom from granting wishes to any *master* who draws the cork?"

She brushed her silvery hair back from her forehead with a delicate hand. "You do not understand the nature of the djinn," she said. "You do not understand the nature of the bottle."

"I understand rank," I said. "On the sea I was between the captain and the rowers. In that house," and I gestured with my head to the palace behind me, "I am below my master and above the kitchen staff. Where are you?"

Her brow furrowed as she thought. "If I work my wonders for centuries, I might at last attain a higher position within the djinn," she said.

It was my turn to smile. "Rank is a game," I said. "It may be conferred by birth, by accident, or by design. But rank does not honor the man. The man honors the rank."

"You are a philosopher," she said, her eyes lightening.

"I am a Greek," I answered. "It is the same thing."

She laughed again, holding her palm over her mouth coquettishly. I could no longer see straight through her, though an occasional piece of driftweed appeared like a delicate tattoo on her skin.

"Perhaps we both need a wish," I said, shifting my weight. One of my feet touched hers and I could feel a slight jolt, as if lightning had run between us. Such things happen occasionally on the open sea.

"Alas, I cannot wish, myself," she said in a whisper. "I can only grant wishes."

I looked at her lovely face, washed with its sudden sadness, and whispered back, "Then I give my wish to you."

She looked directly into my eyes, and I could see her eyes turn golden in the dusty light. I could at the same time somehow see beyond them, not into the sand or water, but to a different place, a place of whirlwinds and smokeless fire.

"Then, Antithias, you will have wasted a wish," she said. Shifting her gaze slightly, she looked behind me, her eyes opening wide in warning. As she spoke, her body seemed to melt into the air, and suddenly there was a great white bird before me, beating its feathered pinions against my body before taking off towards the sky.

"Where are you going?" I cried.

"To the Valley of Abqar," the bird called. "To the home of my people. I will wait there for your wish, Greek. But hurry. I see both your past and your future closing in behind you."

I turned and, pouring down the stone steps of my master's house, were a half dozen guards and one shrilling eunuch pointing his flabby hand in my direction. They came towards me screaming, though what they were saying I was never to know for their scimitars were raised and my Arabic deserts me in moments of sheer terror.

I think I screamed, I am not sure. But I spun around again towards the sea and saw the bird winging away into a halo of light.

"Take me with you," I cried. "I desire no freedom but by your side."

The bird shuddered as it flew, then banked sharply, and headed back towards me, calling, "Is that your wish, Master?"

A scimitar descended.

"That is my wish," I cried, as the blade bit into my throat.

We have lived now for centuries within the green bottle and Zarifa was right, I had not understood its nature. Inside is an entire world, infinite and ever-changing. The smell of the salt air blows through that world, and we dwell in a house that sometimes overlooks the ocean and sometimes overlooks the desert sands.

Zarifa, my love, is as mutable, neither young nor old, neither soft nor hard. She knows the songs of blind Homer and the poet Virgil, as well as the poems of the warlords of Ayyām al-'Arab. She can sing in languages that are long dead.

And she loves me beyond my wishing, or so she says, and I must believe it for she would not lie to me. She loves me though I have no great beauty, my body bearing a sailor's scars and a slave's scar and this curious blood necklace where the scimitar left its mark. She loves me, she says, for my cynic's wit and my noble heart, that I would have given my wish to her.

So we live together in our ever-changing world. I read now in six tongues besides Greek and Arabic, and have learned to paint and sew. My paintings are in the Persian style, but I embroider like a Norman queen. We learn from the centuries, you see, and we taste the world anew each time the cork is drawn.

So there, my master, I have fulfilled your curious wish, speaking my story to you alone. It seems a queer waste of your one piece of luck, but then most men waste their wishes. And if you are a poet and a storyteller, as you say, of the lineage of blind Homer and the rest, but one who has been blocked from telling more tales, then perhaps my history can speed you on your way again. I shall pick up one of your old books, my master, now that we have a day and a night in this new world. Do you have a favorite I should try—or should I just go to a bookseller and trust my luck? In the last few centuries it has been remarkably good, you see.

PETER IN WONDERLAND

I walked down the path with long strides. Behind me I left the birthday breakfast. It was all I allowed. My parents knew that I spent every birthday by myself, in the back garden. Had done so ever since I was ten. And this was my twenty-fifth birthday. I wasn't about to change.

They knew better than to task me for it. Or for the fact that I was a spinster. That I wrote stories and made a better living at it than my sister and her husband combined. Ministers and their wives rarely make ends meet, though they have a nice old manse not far away, so I get to see their children often, and read my stories to them. Soon enough they will be able to read them by themselves.

I walked slowly on the path, which wound by our

small river. I never hurry. And yet I am always on time. I often think the place adjusts to me, not me to it.

I arrived at the big tree, walked around it once, twice, as if to get the feel of it. Remembered how my sister and I used to play there, read to one another. And then I opened the door to the rabbit hole that our gardener, George (now long dead), had built for me.

"Better that than falling down it," he had offered in his gruff voice that disguised what a lovely old man he was. "And stairs for the first few steps down. Till you catch your breath," he'd said.

Even this many years later, I wondered if he had ever climbed down all the way himself. Walked into Wonderland. Talked to the roses. He'd been the only person who even half believed me. He never mentioned going down the hole into magic, nor did I ever ask.

The door creaked open, and the vast darkness below looked up at me. Not a welcome exactly. But it *would* be, once I began.

I sat down, turned onto my stomach, put my legs over the side of the hole, and felt for the first step. There were five in all, and after that, I would fall. But it was a controlled fall, so I was not worried. And there were always the projecting shelves to grab hold of.

I shut the door—always the most difficult part of the trip—and then started down.

Those steps, so familiar, and then the first shelf. I took my time, because there was always something new on each one. Often a teapot, or a biscuit, occasionally a brass thingamabob. Or a tiger's tooth. Once I had found a small bunny, shivering, hungry, and afraid. I had put it in my pocket until we were down on solid ground, where it took off quickly, into the rose garden.

I was down to the tenth shelf when a sudden shaft of light flooded part of the tunnel from above.

This had never happened before. Not even when the White Rabbit had been hopping about. He was always careful not to intrude when I was entering Wonderland.

I heard a creak on the first and second step, and then a rather pleasant voice call out, "What the Devil . . . !" And something—someone—fell down the shaft.

Instinctively, I reached out, and caught the edge of a collar before the young man—for so the voice and the swear had warned me—was stopped in medias res, denying gravity and hanging by the grace of my grip.

"Put your hand on one of the shelves," I said calmly. "They will hold you until you get the feel of the winds."

"Who are you?" he challenged, for of course he could not see me, and he was already beginning to choke up because of the collar tightening around his neck.

"Introductions later," I said reasonably, and he took it so. Reaching out a hand, he found a shelf and balanced there for a bit. I loosed his collar and he gave a short grunt.

Then, I let go of the shelf I'd been clutching, and settled into the comfortable arms of the wind. As I went past him, I said in a gentle voice, "Let go and think of the Queen."

"Which queen?" he asked, which was actually a far more sensible question than he knew.

"Of England," I said, not knowing if he was familiar with any other.

He laughed pleasantly and did as I said, landing in Wonderland a half beat after I did. I had not even time to pat my hair down or order my skirts when he was by my side.

"Wizard!" he said.

I laughed.

"Was that funny?"

"Considering the circumstances," I told him, "very."

I led him down the flower path into the rose garden. "Be careful," I said. "If you speak to the roses impolitely, they *will* prick you!"

"As if roses understand speech!" he said, rather loudly. "Ouch!" quickly followed. "Sorry."

I shook my head. "I *did* warn you."

He looked at me quizzically, as if measuring my mind. "I suppose they speak, too."

"And sing," I said, just as the entire row closest to us broke out into an old Irish air, and right after into gales of laughter.

"I guess I had better listen to you," he said. "In the matters of this Wonderland."

"Perhaps other things as well," I said, but my smile took away the sting of it, and he laughed gently, which was a kind of promise.

He put his hand out, "I am Peter. Thanks for saving me twice."

I took his hand. It was cool, not sweaty. I hated sweaty palms. "Alice," I said.

"Not THE Alice," he retorted, and I knew at once he had read the Reverend's book about Wonderland, with all its mistakes and misunderstandings.

"Yes, I am THE Alice," I said carefully, "but . . ."

"Wizard, indeed."

"He made stuff up, you know."

"Of course he did. It's a book for children. The Jabberwock with eyes of flame, slithy toves, and all that,"

"Jabberwock's eyes can seem that way—when he's coming after you and hasn't met you yet, or taken your measure," I told him. "As for the toves, I hope you have a knife." I took the one from my bodice to show him.

He retrieved a knife from his pocket, but it was in a sheath. "Will this do?

"Toves are very quick and very determined and will strip the flesh from your ankles before you can bend over and unsheathe that knife. Better keep it out of its binding."

"But Reverend Dodgson . . ."

"Made things up. Made them nicer, cleaner, purer. . . ."

He said nothing for a while and we walked a bit in silence, but a pleasant sort of silence, as comfortable as two old friends, which was decidedly odd, since I had very few friends and none of them old.

Before long we came upon the remains of the latest Mad Hatter tea party, which is to say a table half caved in, a broken teapot, a smashed top hat, and a smattering of uneaten biscuits.

"Is that . . ." he asked.

"Yes," I said. And before I could explain, Chessy arrived, well brushed, smiling down at us with his cat-that-ate-the-canary smile. Or maybe had eaten three.

"Oh," he purred, "it was a smasher this time. I had told Hatter that making more hats would drive him mad. All that mercury, you know. But he was too far gone to listen. And he never did believe in science. So, we lost another mouse—this one a church mouse. I had to send my apologies to the Bishop, who did a dozen Hail Marys in the mouse's honor. Waste of a good mouse, I told him."

"And what of the March Hare?" Peter asked.

"It was already April," said Chessy, as if that explained everything. And then he suddenly disappeared except for his smile. "Alice," said the smile, "could have told you that!" And then the smile was gone, too.

"Curiouser and curiouser," Peter said, turning to me. Then he winked and we both laughed. And that was the most curious thing of all because every one of the young men my parents had introduced me to had no sense of humor. Nor did they read. Only the Bible and the daily papers. It made them very dull. All of them too sensible for my liking. There was nothing dull about this Peter.

Peter swiped the only two unsmashed biscuits, handing me one of them. "I suppose tea is out of the question?"

Just then Caterpillar materialized, wearing a bright blue tam with *Go Scotland!* embroidered upon it and smoking his ever-ready hookah. He had a table laid before him with three steaming cups of tea and lovely violet-painted serviettes. "It is the very best Indian tea I could find at such short notice," he said. "Alice, introduce me to your young man."

"He's not mine . . ." I began, but Peter nodded as if seeing a seven-foot caterpillar dressed in a tam were an everyday event, "I am Peter Wallace," he said. "Miss Liddell and I have just started an acquaintance." He winked at me.

That he already knew my last name without my telling it was very suspicious, and I supposed Mummy or Daddy had put him up to it. But I forgave him that small omission.

"Well stated, and well played, young Wallace," Caterpillar said. "I am Pillar and accept your invitation to the wedding."

"Whoa . . ." I interjected. "By *just started*, Mr. Wallace means we met an hour ago. In the rabbit hole."

"An hour in Wonderland, as you very well know, dear Alice, can be a century elsewhere." Caterpillar gave a shudder which ran up and down his long body.

That was always his reaction to even thinking about Elsewhere, which he brought up once in every conversation I have ever had with him.

"Or an eyeblink," I said unamused. "You are worse than my parents, Pillar."

"Or better," he said. "It's just a matter of observation. Besides, that boy has 'keeper' written all over him."

I didn't know if he meant some sort of sportsman, or boyfriend, or husband. I decided to ignore both Caterpillar and Peter. I turned away and stared across the meadow. And lucky I did so, otherwise I might not have seen the quartet of slithy toves slithering through the grass.

"TOVES!" I shouted and pointed with one hand, while fumbling in my bodice with the other for my knife, and suddenly feeling embarrassed about doing so, which made the fumbling take even longer.

Suddenly the toves were around us, and my knife only partially drawn.

With quick strikes, Peter took out three of them, one after another, and I took out the fourth, but just barely. We looked at one another in a kind of dazed amazement, and had hardly a moment to take a deep breath, when there was a roar.

"Jabberwocky, I suppose?" Peter asked. His voice seemed untroubled.

"Of course. He can smell dead toves a mile away. I will give him my one. You give him your three."

"Why don't you give him all of them?" Peter asked

sensibly. "He trusts you. He doesn't know me."

"He can smell the bloods on your knife and mine. He is already aware of which is which."

"Oh!" said Peter, "I understand now."

And so we did.

As usual, Jabber turned his back while eating, knowing that he was a sloppy eater at best and a boor at worst. He did not want to submit his friends to it. Mostly, I think, for fear it could turn them against him. He had obviously never seen some of the young men I was forced to eat with at dinner parties.

When he was done, I offered him a large handkerchief which I always carry with me just for such occasions. And then there were introductions all around.

Peter remarked, "I have read about you and am in awe of your prowess."

Jabber sniffled about, scratched in the dirt with one claw, and said, "Pshaw, Peter, I do no more than the average dragon."

Peter replied, "I have known dragons in my day, and you are top of the list."

I think my mouth dropped. "You have known dragons?"

"I come from a long line of them. Wait until you meet my great-grandmother."

Jabber snuffled a bit more, and then, still a bit teary,

said, "The queens are having a dinner and live performance. I hope you might like to accompany me. Both of you."

"Wizard!" said Peter, but I was more cautious. "What kind of performance? Not one of her Off-with-your-head acts? Once is enough. Twice was too much. I prefer not . . ."

"Something rather special, I think," said Jabber. "There's to be pink champagne. Or it may be just peach juice. One never knows. The Duchess is in charge."

"Then it will be the juice," I told Peter. "If the Duchess is in charge."

"I'd rather keep my head in both instances," he said. "Champers always does me in after a single glass."

"Me, too," I said, surprised a young man would admit as much. "Even half a glass. I have no head for it."

We followed Jabber back.

"Best we keep close," I told Peter. "Where the Red Queen sits changes with her every whim, but he has a great nose, and usually knows right where she is. Since he is her champion, that's a good nose to have!"

"A good nose, indeed," said Peter. "Should I keep an eye out for more of those toves as we go along?"

"No, they only fight once a day. And as we wiped out their entire corps, it will be some time before they are ready, and we will be long gone by then."

"*We?*" he said. "I am beginning to like it here."

"It gets very worrying the second day onward," I admitted. "And if I am gone more than the afternoon of my birthday, there will be policemen searching the grounds and possibly discovering the door into Wonderland."

"It's your birthday? But I have nothing to give you, Alice," he said, making a fancy bow he probably had learned in dancing school.

"Then try not to lose your head here in Wonderland," I told him. "The Red Queen rather likes to threaten that all the time, and once in a blue moon she actually does it." I sighed and said something that surprised me more than Peter. "I . . . I rather like your head. So that's my birthday present—that you keep it on your shoulders."

"Not my head," he said, "I haven't lost that, but I am afraid I've lost a rather a different part . . ."

"Please don't speak of it. Not yet." I was suddenly aflutter, and knew bad choices often came with flutters. It was how my sister was married. It is not a good pairing at all.

"I shall be silent till you tell me to speak," he said, placing his right-hand pointer finger across his mouth.

We walked onto a path strewn with rosebuds that were notable for their silence, then across a long meadow as thick as a carpet. And there ahead of us sat the Red

Queen and the White Queen on the very top of a three-tiered platform. Below them, in order of importance, was the full court.

The White Rabbit, in full mufti, stood in front of the tiers, holding a certificate. There was black ink across the front of both his paws. And that gave *me* pause. It must have been a very recent proclamation.

I turned and looked at Peter's head. It *was* a very nice head. I would do anything to keep it on his shoulders. They looked like strong, comfortable, comforting shoulders.

"If I say 'Turn around, and run like the wind back to the rabbit hole,' will you do so?" I whispered.

"Not without you," he said.

And at that I wondered if it was two heads the Red Queen was after.

The White Rabbit cleared his throat. "Hmmmmm, ladies and gentlefolk of all persuasions," he said, then looked up at the sky. We all looked up as well. Chessy smiled above us.

"We are here," said the White Rabbit, "on a solemn occasion, for it is rare that a young Princess of Wonderland—"

"AHEM . . . !" It was the Red Queen clearing her throat. "No one with a head still on is a princess here."

"That a young woman of the outer world . . ." the White Rabbit corrected quickly.

"Good enough," said the queen, "you may go on."

The White Rabbit nodded. "And her consort—"

"Wait a minute . . ." Both Peter and I spoke as one.

The White Rabbit glanced at the Red Queen, who waved him aside and stood.

Fearing what might come next, the White Rabbit dropped the scroll, got down on all fours, and took off in the direction of the rabbit hole. In twenty steps he was hidden from sight, but not from sound because he was puffing like a freight train bound for its final station.

The Knave of Hearts picked up the scroll and carried it to the top tier, where he handed it to the White Queen, who passed it over to the Red Queen, who looked at it once, twice, and then called out in stentorian tones, "Bring in the wedding meats!"

The wedding meats—an old flamingo and a young stoat—stood trembling before them. Then in walked the Royal Executioner with a very large sword.

"Run!" I whispered loudly to Peter. But he did not run. Instead he moved forward and said, "Oh noble queen, I eat no meats and such an execution would spoil any wedding I might have."

"Nonsense!" said the Queen. "Everyone eats meat."

"Not the White Rabbit," I ventured.

"Nor the Flamingo," Peter added.

"Fish," the Flamingo offered in a trembling voice.

"Shut up!" Peter hissed. Then he called up to the queen once again. "But high tea with jam sandwiches would be just the treat for my bride and me. And then we must dash away for our honeymoon."

"Honeymoon . . ." everyone in the meadow repeated in highly excited tones.

As soon as we had gulped down jam sandwiches and swallowed a cup of tea each, Peter and I raced away, holding hands, which, under the circumstances, felt very nice.

And two years later, when we got into a Rolls to drive off to our real honeymoon, it felt even nicer.

"Is that a true story, Mummy?" asked Owen, who was the oldest of our three.

"Cross my heart and . . ." I went no further.

"Can we go to Wonderland, too?" the twins asked.

"As soon as you are old enough and strong enough to carry a knife and your father says it is all right to do so."

"All right to do what?" It was Peter who had come in from his writing room in the garden house.

"To go to Wonderland," the three children cried.

"As soon as you turn ten," he said. "And your mother and I will accompany you."

As Owen was six and the twins both four, that seemed long enough away.

I said as much to Peter in the evening, after the children were in bed and after he read me his latest Wonderland poem, the last one for his new book.

"They will forget by then," Peter said. "Or perhaps it is time to fill in that old rabbit hole. We haven't been back in years." But his eyes got a bit watery when he said that, as did mine. After all, without Wonderland, we wouldn't have been able to live Happily Ever After.

And after all, it was an adventure we couldn't deny our own darling children, no matter what the grandparents might think!

And old Reverend Dodgson, that old dodderer in his nineties, fully agreed.

THE EROTIC IN FAERIE

THE FOOTNOTES

From the paper by Dr. Jane Yolen, given at the Hundredth Anniversary of the International Society to Preserve the Fey.

The Paper itself has disappeared (written in Invisible Ink) and only the footnotes remain. One might wonder why. It is because they alone were typed.

Still, by themselves, the footnotes give the careful reader a taste of what the original thesis must have been, and why it is such a disaster that the thesis has been lost to us forever.

1. Is this what Wallace Stegner means in his felicitous phrase, "The Geography of Hope?"

2. Though he adds, ". . . fairyland arouses a longing (in the reader) for what he knows not . . ." Lewis, with his own problems vis-à-vis the erotic, was certainly not making the connection here. Indeed he *absolutely* knew not.

3. As is well-known in the Carmina Burana: Larve, Fauni, Manes, Nymphe, Sirene, Hamadriades, Satyri, Incubi, Penates.

4. What could be clearer.? T. S. Eliot even noted it. Mermaids, indeed. "Singing, each to each. . . ." needing, in other words, no help from male mer to conceive. Prufrock is not the only love song Eliot attempted, though one needs to be prepared to go deep to tease out his actual meanings. Not everyone is willing to stick with his maunderings that long.

5. Shakespeare, too, emphasized the popular misconceptions of conception, and what happens in the erotic whenever the fey lend a hand. "And bootless make the breathless housewife churn" is one. Another: "Fright the maidens in the villagery." A third: "Mislead the night-wanderers."

6. Ellen Kushner's fairyland is a place of connubial delight as well, and surely she should know.

7. Not unlike the Irish love-talker, the vaunted Gan-

canagh, who appears with a pipe in Irish ballads, making love to young women who afterwards pine away with love for him.

8. Likewise the Scottish water horse who steals away young women for what at first appears as romance, and ends in their deaths. He eats their flesh, sucks the marrow from their bones. A kind of fairy love guru, but certainly not a gourmet.

9. Anne Rice, on the other hand, bludgeons the reader with the sensual and her Faerie always smells of the boudoir after the Act. Or the abattoir.

10. But isn't it always thus: the fey and human consume as they consummate. No one gets out of faerie entirely alive.

STORY NOTES AND POEMS

Sans Soleil

First published in 1976, in my second original fairytale collection, *Moon Ribbon*. I needed to balance the happy fairy tales with some dark and/or simply sad stories. It reminds me in style and substance of the many Oscar Wilde fairy tales I had read both as a child and again as an adult, when I understood the deep pathos beneath even the lightest of his stories.

The poem was written for *The Scarlet Circus* and published here first.

The Punishment of the Sun

My two sons, fair-haired blue-eyed,
had no friend in the sun.

Like their father, they bathed
in lotion, sought the shadows,
lingered long under trees.
My daughter, dark as I am
could laze without danger.
It is a fairy tale of sorts,
a skin, not a skein
of warning, memory,
and relief.

Dusty Loves

This was one of three of my published short stories about the Shouting Fey: "The Thirteenth Fey," "The Uncorking of Uncle Finn," and "Dusty Loves." The first one turned into the novel *Curse of the Thirteenth Fey*, a reworking of Sleeping Beauty from the fairy's point of view.

As for the poem, it was written a number of years ago for a verse novel about Sleeping Beauty that I have never finished.

All the Same

The bones of princes
And the bones of servants
All look the same in the hedge.

Thin, white, fined-down,
Silent mottoes, eternal twigs
That do not change color in the Fall.

I pinch my hand and feel
Small bones beneath
The fragile shield of skin.

We do not go dust to dust
As the book tells us,
But bone to bone.

The hedge holds us together,
Bound to eternity,
Bonded, and bare.

Unicorn Tapestry

Written for and published in my *Here There Be Unicorns* collection (part of a series that began with *Here There Be Dragons* and went on to unicorns, ghosts, witches, etc). A different kind of unicorn story, because I had already written the hardcore unicorn tales for the collection. I was not expecting it to turn into a love story.

The poem was written in 2020 as part of my poem-a-day project, but this is its first publication.

Virus 20: A Nurse's Advice

Wear a mask and gloves
when you wipe down unicorns.
Discard gloves after use
or the unicorns will eat them,
to their detriment.
If you don't have a mask, wear a cod piece.
Be careful using Clorox wipes:
can be toxic to the pixies.
Vinegar works well in wiping lettuce,
plus a bit of a whine.
Newspapers should be set aside
a month before opening.
'Tis best for your digestion.
If you can't find Purell,
veggie soap is good
and still on the shelves,
but do not eat it
or inject it.
Humans are not meant to be so clean.
Keep the house fairies in,
the garden fairies out.
Blow your nose on a leaf
or use it for toilet paper
as long as it is not poison ivy,
or nettles. Dock helps.
Unsolicited advice:
take it for what it's worth.

Remember to let the unicorns go.
They do not housebreak easily.
Your carpets and tapestries
will be the worse for their wear.

A Ghost of an Affair

This story was first published in a collection of mine called *Sister Emily's Lightship* in 2000. The story was written when I was in Scotland one summer, where I own a house near the coast of Fife, not far from Crail where the story is set. I had begun it several years earlier for a ghost anthology, but hadn't discovered its true plot in time (a problem I often have!). But when I did, the story took mere days to finish. Re-reading still makes me tear up.

As for the poem, it is true and somehow replicates the story. This poem was written in 2020 and celebrates something that happened in that year. Right before the virus shut down the world, I re-met a man from my past (we had dated two months in college). We met again when I was a fifteen-year widow, he a five-year widower. Yes, magic can still happen.

Meeting in Time

We slept side by side,

hands to ourselves,
college kids who hadn't a clue.
We knew one another for two months,
married others,
and after their long deaths,
re-met, this time for certain.
It's about time.
I draw the curtain.

Reader, I married him.

Dark Seed, Dark Stone

This story was first published in *Realms of Fantasy* in 2002, when the magazine was still alive and well. The story began with a first line, but I had not a clue as to where it was heading. But I followed the thread of it, never expecting it would turn into a love story. Sometimes these things happen. Just as they do in real life!

The poem was written in 2020, as I write a poem a day and send them out to over a thousand subscribers. This is its first publication.

Gravestones

I read gravestones
the way other people read books

to find out how things began,
how they ended.
I read with my eyes
and fingers,
taking the mold of the letters,
the insights of serif.
But I make up the in-between.
I do not need to know the actual.
Everyone has an actual.
But they also each have a secret truth.
That's what I want to read.
and so, I write it myself.

Dragonfield

I wrote this story back in the mid-1980s. At a time when I was tired of the mightily thewed, over-muscled hero figures. I wanted one who was a bit more of a grifter, and yet could be turned into a good man with the help and guidance of a strong female. The story turned into the title story of a collection of mine, and some years later I rewrote it for a graphic novel with gorgeous sequential art by Rebecca Guay, who lived close by and became a dear friend.

The poem accompanying this story was first published in my band's first (and only) CD in 2018, but it had been written in 2014 and appeared in *Myth &*

Moor, a small but intense online zine by Terri Windling—author, editor, and illustrator.

Hero's Thumb

Once even the whorls were huge,
like unexplored worlds
before we cut them down,
sandblasted their mountains,
gentrified their woods.

Once, even the nail was powerful,
shining like polished agate,
before we smashed it into sparkles
to paste on book covers,
or a child's pretend crown.

Once the knuckle flexed
supple as a wire walker
between twin towers,
well before the hatred
brought them down.

Lately, the hero's thumb
has grown slow, cranky,
crackling, flamed,
numbed by arthritis,
that courier of age.

It cannot hold the bowstring,
curl the mead cup,
clap the bull dancers,
praise the gods,
salute the high king.

It just waits to be folded,
hand upon stilled chest,
laid onto the funerary,
Ithaka long over,
a new journey to begin.

The Sword and the Stone

First appeared in *The Magazine of Fantasy and Science Fiction* (F&SF), then in 1986 in my collection of my Arthurian stories, *Merlin's Booke*. It probably came about because as a child, my brother Steve, my best friend Diane, and I played King Arthur in Central Park across from our apartment building, and I was the only one who had read the books about King Arthur. I refused to be Guinevere in our games. Too sappy. So unheroic. So, in this story I have written a Guinevere I might have accepted playing.

As for this poem, it was written for *Scarlet Circus*.

<u>The Girl Speaks to the Mage</u>

Do not have expectations,
nor make of me enchantments.
I do not cook dinners,
nor do I weave or sew.
I embroider stories,
make masques,
can lift a sword
to plunge it into stone.
My heart loves where it will.
I speak five languages,
or at least I know the word NO
in every one of them.
I wear a small dirk in my bodice,
a small smirk on my mouth.
If that makes me a new kind of girl,
one who speaks truth to the powerful,
warns them against their old, sodden ways,
that is the only magic I shall ever wield.
You get one warning.
This is it.

The Sea Man

I have written quite a few stories and books about mermaids, and very few about mermen. But this novella began when I was researching for a book about sea myths and folktales (*The Fish Prince and Other Stories*, written with Shulamith Oppenheim for Interlink Publishers). During my research, I came upon a piece that spoke of a seventeenth century Dutch Navy captain's log which detailed an encounter with a "sea man." Whether I believed the log or not, a story of my own began. It took me several years to get a handle on it. The finished story was way too long and too sophisticated for a picture book. It finally turned into a small book, actually a novella, *The Sea Man*, illustrated with line drawings by Christopher Denise. Though it is now long out of print, I love it to this day and am happy to have it back in circulation.

The poem is part of an as-yet unfinished verse novel, "The Mermaid Corps," and published here for the first time.

An Old Story About the Mer

A lonely wife sits on a rock,
waiting for her husband
to return from a voyage.
She suspects he has wives
in other ports but does not care.
One evening, a merman
sees her on the rock,
leaps up to sit by her,
his green tail curling around her
with a possessiveness her husband

has never shown.
He cannot speak above the water.
The mer have no tongues.
They speak below the waves
with their hands,
a fluid syncopation.
Above the waves they feel clumsy,
though they look to humans
as mobile as the waves themselves.
He tells the woman of her beauty.
He is used to speaking such lies.
All women are beautiful
to a merman.
So, it is only a half step
from the truth.
At dawn he signals her to follow,
and dives into the sea.
She takes a lone long glance
out to the ocean,
where there is no hint
of her husband's ship,
and pulling her skirts around her
she jumps awkwardly into the sea.
The sea crowns her with bubbles.
Little fish swim between her fingers.
The merman sucks the marrow
From the drowned woman's bones.

Memoirs of a Bottle Djinn

I was asked to write a story by my dear friend Susan Shwartz for a fantasy/SF anthology she was editing, about love stories, or women's issues, or both. And there it appeared. Why a Djinn story? It popped into my head, almost fully formed, which is not usual with me. Perhaps Susan suggested I do something exotic. Or perhaps she said "erotic" and I heard "exotic." Either way—MBD happened rather easily. And taken quickly for her anthology, as I recall.

The poem below was written for this book and first published here. It is *not* true. Remember, I am both a poet and a storyteller. My father was a storyteller, too. Only his were just lies.

<u>That Old Bottle</u>

My father kept an old bottle of gin
in the backstairs cupboard.
"It's magic," he said.
"Best leave it alone."
I thought he meant
a *djinn* lived there, her hair dark,
holding mysteries.
I was a fairy-tale reader,
a believer at a young age.
I opened the top one day,
when my father was at work.

Turned the bottle upside down,
hoping to make her acquaintance,
hoping to learn magic, find beauty.
I didn't care which.
I was doused with gin.
When he came home,
My father took a switch to my backside.
I learned silence and mystery then,
and story.
Two sides of the magic coin.

Peter in Wonderland

As we were putting together this collection of stories, my editor/publisher said, "Please write a new story for it." I sighed. For some time I had been writing poetry, nonfiction, picture books, and novels galore, but I hadn't written a new story in years. (Though I have close to 300 published short stories in my history!) But I like my editor/publisher. So, I said yes.

And then I wandered about like some old Victorian poet, seeking an Idea. When Wonderland waved its hand at me, I thought to give Alice another trip down there. And then Peter (who is my new husband after fifteen years of widowhood) tumbled in, too.

And after three days of thinking about the story and what could happen in it, I wrote it in a single sitting. Revised it the next day (mostly to get rid of extra commas and delete bad spelling) and sent it on. I quite like it, and hope you do, too. Must think about writing some more short stories in the near future. If I can find another Idea.

Unlike the story, this is a poem I wrote in 2020. But I think it matches the tale I have told quite well.

Always Mimsy

It was, Alice thought,
another Mimsy day.
Wonderland often promises,
but does not always keep
such promises firmly in mind.
So, this day, like most English mid-weeks,
was moist and weep-knit,
and the chorus of roses
shrieked in their beauty.
Rabbits took turn with watches,
making certain things were ship-shape.
Their badges all said:
Hare Today, Gone Tomorrow.
She noticed the empty table in the woods.
Clearly the Mad Hatter was homeless once again,
which meant no one was caring
for the dear little dormouse.
She would have to report it to the authorities.
But if there was one thing always to be sure of,
it was the Jabberwock,

so, she kept her vorpal blade close to hand,
and her cell phone on the police band.
Sometimes the blade worked,
often it did not.
After all, in Wonderland,
things were always Mimsy.

The Erotic in Faerie: The Footnotes

This was meant for a small, personally published pamphlet/anthology by Emma Bull, but the anthology never happened, so this is the piece's first publication. As someone who has a master's degree in education and six honorary doctorates, I have read my fill of slightly snarky footnotes about books of poetry and prose. I think the footnotes in my piece only exaggerate slightly!

On the other hand, the poem—written in 2028 but never before published—is not from the educator's POV, but the students and other poets! It is published here for the first time.

Chaucer's Nightmare

"When that Aprill" . . . the poet wrote
in his medieval cursive,
not knowing that students
by the millions, would curse his name.

Footnotes, like lice,
would grow in his hair.
And the universe
(as well as universities)
would feel the weight
of theses in their libraries,
and the hard parsing
of his English till the end of time.
We lesser poets
take our chances,
welcoming the burden
of history's anointment.
When that May . . .
I begin, hoping for the best.

Jane Yolen (*Owl Moon*, *The Midnight Circus*, the How Do Dinosaurs? series)'s four hundredth book came out in 2020, and she is starting the new count with *Arch of Bone*—with her eye on five hundred! She has been writing and publishing since the early sixties, when she sold her first book (about female pirates) on her twenty-second birthday. But Yolen began her publishing career as a journalist (short-lived) and as an editor (longer-lived), for Knopf and Harcourt, in the children's department.

Yolen graduated from Smith College in Northampton, Massachusetts, with an MEd (master's degree in education) from the University of Massachusetts, Amherst. She has six honorary doctorates for her body of work. She was the first woman to give the Andrew Lang lecture at the University of St Andrews in Scotland, in a lecture series that began in 1927. Yolen was also president for two years of the Science Fiction Writers of America, and on the board of the Society of Children's Book Writers for forty-five years.

Yolen's books and stories have won three World Fantasy Awards, two Nebula Awards, three Mythopoeic Awards, two Christopher Medals, three SCBWI awards, the Massachusetts Book Center Award, two Golden Kite Awards, and a Caldecott Medal, as well as many others. She was nominated in 2020 by the United States for the Astrid Lindgren Memorial Award. She was the first Western Mass author to win a New England Public Radio Arts and Humanities Award.

Yolen has also received awards from both the Jewish Book Council and the Catholic Book Council, making her very ecumenical. Her award from the New England Science Fiction Association set her good coat on fire, which she takes as a lesson about the dangers of awards.

Yolen lives in Western Massachusetts and St Andrews, Scotland.

Brandon Sanderson is a *New York Times* bestselling fantasy and science fiction author. His series works include Mistborn, the Stormlight Archive, Infinity Blade, Legion, Skyward, and more. Brandon has sold more than twenty-one million books internationally. In 2007, he was chosen to finish Robert Jordan's iconic The Wheel of Time series. In 2022, his record-breaking Kickstarter raised more than $40 million. Brandon lives in Utah with his family.

Extended Copyright

Fiction, edited by Edward L. Ferman. December 1985.

"The Sea Man" copyright © 1997 by Jane Yolen. First appeared in *The Sea Man* (Philomel Books: New York City).

"Memoirs of a Bottle Djinn" copyright © 1988 by Jane Yolen. First appeared in *Arabesques*, edited by Susan Shwartz (Avon Books: New York).

"Peter in Wonderland" copyright © 2023 by Jane Yolen. Original to this collection.

"The Erotic in Faerie: The Footnotes" copyright © 2023 by Jane Yolen. Original to this collection.

Poetry

"The Punishment of the Sun" copyright © 2023 by Jane Yolen. Original to this collection.

"All the Same" copyright © 2023 by Jane Yolen. Original to this collection.

"Virus 20: A Nurse's Advice" copyright © 2023 by Jane Yolen. Original to this collection.

"Meeting in Time" copyright © 2020 by Jane Yolen. First published to Jane Yolen's poetry mailing list.